the lover in my dreams

Shivani Singhal

Srishti
PUBLISHERS & DISTRIBUTORS

Srishti Publishers & Distributors
A unit of AJR Publishing LLP
212A, Peacock Lane
Shahpur Jat, New Delhi – 110 049
editorial@srishtipublishers.com

First published by
Srishti Publishers & Distributors in 2021

10 9 8 7 6 5 4 3 2 1

Printed and bound in India

Prologue

"Hello? Ruby? Please, I need you. I'll die... please come to meet me," I sob into the phone.

"Are you okay? Naina, what happened?" Ruby panics.

"I have no idea what is happening to me. I am going mad," I explode over the phone.

"Relax, baby! Come on, breathe in, and breathe out. Everything is going to be fine."

She's trying to calm me. She is not getting it. I have tried a hell lot of ways to calm myself down already. But nothing is working.

"I need to see a psychiatrist. I am losing my mind!" I howl.

"Baby, I spoke with you a week ago when you came back from your honeymoon. You were so happy. What has happened in a week?" Ruby asks.

"I lied!" I break down. I snivel.

Part - 1

Three-and-a-half months ago…

1

"Nainaaaa, c'mon out. We are getting late," Tanvi bellows from outside the washroom cabin.

"Yeah, baby. Coming. Give me a minute!" I scream right back.

"Oh my god! It looks so good on you." Tanvi gasps, her hands covering her mouth. I step outside the cabin.

"You know that you are a bitch for buying this dress. I'll hate you for this, always," Tanvi teases.

I check myself in the big mirror. It's true; I look ravishing. My curves stand out perfectly in this taut dress, with my legs looking shimmery. I'm killing it.

"I am in love with this dress!" I exclaim and turn to Tanvi.

"I saw it first," she replies curtly, digging her forefinger into my love handle.

"Stop it! Nooo!" I spank her on the shoulder.

"C'mon, girls!" Tiger enters the girls' restroom, and Tanvi imitates him right back, "C'mon, girls."

Ruby comes in too, and shoots the three of us a stern look. "I sent you in here to bring them out. But you're such a girl," Ruby twits at Tiger.

"Oh, please!" Tiger retorts in his delicate tone. "I just came here to call them. You are the one who was busy putting lipstick on your camel-like lips." He is always like this – very sensitive, compared to the other rugged boys his age.

Ruby thumps him hard on his shoulder.

"You are one insensitive bitch!" he squawks at Ruby rubbing his shoulder and strides out.

"Why do you behave so rudely with him? He never says anything mean to you," Tanvi frowns at Ruby, storming out behind Tiger.

Ruby makes a face. I chortle, taking my lipstick and compact out of my purse as Ruby joins me at the mirror.

All four of us finally leave for the lounge bar in Ruby's car, a shining black Skoda Superb. She is our wealthiest friend, and is very genial and kind. I am sitting in the front passenger seat, while she is driving, and Tanvi and Tiger are dancing in the back. Both of them are the clowns of our group, but truthfully, also the gems.

Tanvi is a tomboy, short in height with short and slightly curly hair falling onto her shoulders. She is lean and an absolute loudspeaker. Tiger is lanky, and very gentle in everything he does.

Both of the idiots are singing along to 'Something just like this...' as it plays on the stereo. I've plugged my ears with my forefingers while Ruby is yelling at them to stop.

The ride proceeds, and we finally arrive at our destination – our favourite lounge bar in Connaught Place.

We order our usuals. We had come here on Friday but I'd urged everyone to come here again today, because I know this is the only month I can visit this place as often as I want. After that, I don't know where I will be; where my destiny will take me.

I gaze around with a longing to just keep coming back here, as often as I come now with my buffoons. I don't want things to change. It seems too soon for everything to change.

"Heyiiiiiii!" Tanvi bellows in my left ear.

"Are you mad?" Ah! She's made me temporarily deaf.

"Where are you lost?" Tanvi asks, putting her arm around my neck.

"You know, it is the only month we have left, to come here together," I reply, crestfallen.

"Why? Are you dying? We will all keep catching up here," Ruby interjects.

"Oh, you bimbo! Why would she die, or any of us?" squawks Tanvi.

"She didn't mean it in that sense." I try to calm Tanvi down.

I have very little time left to spend with my friends. So, as much time as I do have, I want to spend it merrily.

Ruby makes a face at Tanvi, and turns her head busily to her phone.

"Why are your parents doing this to you?" Tiger says from across the table, venting his frustration. "It is the f**king twenty-first century. What world do they live in?"

"Wow! Now, you are talking like a man," Ruby twits at Tiger. She spares a moment away from her phone's screen to look at him.

"Oh, shut up! I am pretty serious here," protests Tiger.

"You used the word 'pretty'?" Ruby teases him again.

"I hate you," Tiger croaks, then gets up to amble towards the boy's restroom.

"Leave them. Can't you talk to your mom or your brother about it?" Tanvi asks me affectionately.

"Nope. When it comes to me, they all become one. Everything related to my life is decided by them. You know how much I tried to convince them to let me apply for the college placement. But they didn't agree. Now, I will do as they ask and just get done with it."

"It is your f**king life. You can't just sit like this and let them make f**king decisions for you. It is you, and only you, who should decide for yourself," Tanvi grows agitated.

"I know," I reply. "But who has made all my decisions up until now? What I will wear? Whether I'll cut my hair or not? Or put on makeup or not? Everything is sanctioned by them. Now, I have given up, bro. I can't fight anymore, because it is always me who gets hurt in the end." I've gotten tired of talking about this topic, because I know that nothing is going to change.

As the evening continues, we all drink, gorge on food and dance a little. In time, I head to the restroom to change my clothes. I put on my casual clothes over my dress.

It is now 5.30 and I have to reach home before 6. I am not allowed to stay out after six.

Euphorically, we all head back home. Tanvi is hammered. While riding back home, I warned them not to miss a single day of college till the exams. I want to cherish every special moment of college with them.

Whenever I am with them, but I forget about all my worries. And when I reach home, sadness and frustration envelope me. I hate to be home, but I bid them goodbye.

My mom starts complaining from the moment I walk in through the door. "Where were you, Naina? You know your papa doesn't like you staying out till late." Her remark immediately washes away my hangover, and fills me with exasperation.

"Late? It is five minutes past six," I growl and walk straight to my room.

"You are mulish," she shoots back. "I don't know how you will get settled after marriage. We tolerate this behaviour because you are our daughter, but let me tell you, your in-laws will not be this patient with you. Then, you will miss us and understand that we were right." She follows me to my room, nagging.

I shut myself inside the washroom.

My entire family is desperate to prove one thing to me – that whatever they are doing with me is right, and that one day I will understand this. But if they are so sure about being right, then why are they so desperate to prove it to me? And aren't they unintentionally wishing a bad future upon me by wanting to prove this? Oh yes, I will have such bad in-laws that I will miss my parents, and think that all those restrictions they put on me were right. So, in a way, they are preparing me to bear the future torture by my in-laws.

Tears begin to well up in my eyes. I have grown quite emotional, because there is only a month left of college... then, I will be caged inside this house. Papa is very orthodox. According to him, girls should stay inside the house. And as if that wasn't enough, he is now all set to get me hitched.

My profile has been created on all the match-making websites. Papa has also paid money to various agents in the match-making industry to send us good *rishtas*.

Soon, I will be betrothed to someone. And I'll not be asked for my approval, not once.

Mummy knocks on the washroom door, interrupting my thoughts. "Naina, open the door. It is urgent. Your papa is asking for you."

My heartbeat races in my chest. Now what does he want to talk about?

I go to his room and stand docilely, announcing my presence with a quiet, curt, "Yes, Papa?"

He looks at me, and a broad smile appears on his lips.

"Guruji is coming," he says. "He is coming all the way from Jammu to Delhi, especially for us. He will spend a night at our place. I want you to serve him and his disciples with all your heart. You have always been very lucky in your life. Whose blessings helped you to get all this? He told you to keep the Monday fasts, so that all the troubles in your life vanish by the blessings of Lord Shiva."

I nod like an obedient daughter, and listen to him standing beside Neeraj bhaiya.

"All the things that I have in my life today are because of his blessings. He bestowed me with a good job, a goddess-like wife, and kids like you two." Papa starts lauding Guruji again. We hear this speech every month. He is an ardent follower of Guruji.

"If he blesses you both, then your lives will be set," he continues. "Now, the only things I wish for in my life are that you get a perfect job, and your sister, a suitable groom. Your mom and I will bathe in the Ganga then..." Please, somebody stop him.

"You will both have to take care of their every need. Naina, you will make *sattvic bhojan* for them, and also all types of sweets, everything at home."

After taking note of all the instructions from Papa, I come straight to my room. Guruji and his disciples, god knows how many disciples, will arrive by tomorrow evening. I'll have to start with the preparations early the next morning.

So, this means no college for two days! Why does he have to come tomorrow? Couldn't he have waited just a month? I would have done the preparations wholeheartedly then.

2

"Nainaaaaa, your cell phone is ringing!" Mom shouts.

This always happens. Whenever Guruji is about to visit our place, everything becomes a tornado of clutter and chaos. Now, who is calling me? Ah, it's Bhavya. What does she want?

"Hello," I hear her cooing from the other line, "how is my sweet little sister?"

"Hello," I say, "I am good. Was a little busy." I know she won't put the phone down soon.

"When are you not busy? If you haven't noticed, I am the one who just got married. So, I am expected to be busy. Instead, you are always the busy one. But I have many servants here. Bhavesh never lets me do any work."

She never misses a chance to make me feel low. "Okay. What made you call me?" I am grumpy. Since five o'clock in the morning, I've been standing on my feet, making laddoos and jalebis.

"Nothing special. I just wanted you to know that Bhavesh bought me a diamond ring. It is a solitaire. It is worth 1.5 lakhs!" she says rapturously.

"Oh! That's nice. Good for you." Why on earth has she called me to tell this?

"I'll send you a picture. Show it to Taiji and Neeraj bhaiya. You wouldn't have seen such a beautiful ring."

I want to hang up right away, but I can't. If I do, she will sulk about it for months. Instead, I drone in reply, "Hmmm."

"I will ask Tauji to find a groom for you who can also buy such an expensive ring. Why would I not wish good for you? You are my sister."

I can't tolerate her crap anymore.

Mummy enters the kitchen and spots me on the phone. "Naina, have you made the jalebis? Who are you chit-chatting with?"

"No, I am making them," I explain. "The batter is ready, I just have to fry them."

"You know there is so much work to do. Guruji can arrive at any moment!" Mummy croaks and leaves the kitchen.

"Bhavya, do you want to talk to Mummy? I am busy right now."

"I called to talk to you," I hear her reply. "What will I say to Taiji? You tell her about my ring. I will do one thing; I will WhatsApp the picture of my solitaire to the family group."

Is she a madwoman?

"So, Guruji is coming?" she continues. "Is Tauji fixing your marriage? You never tell me anything! I always tell you about every small thing in my life. I even told you that I bought a silk saree last week worth fifty grand." She just doesn't quit.

"Bhavya, Guruji is coming, and he can arrive any time. I have a lot of work. I'll call you tomorrow." I am out of patience.

"At least tell me why he is coming."

"Papa called him," I reply. "My marriage is not being fixed. Whenever it is, I will tell you. And can anything stay hidden from you?" I am getting tired of nestling the phone on my shoulder.

"What do you mean by 'can anything stay hidden from me'?" she says. "Do you think I just gossip on the phone the whole day? Yes, I agree, I have servants to work for me. And I don't even have to cook like you do. But I still have many other important jobs to do. I am a very social person. I have many parties and lunches to go to. But still—"

"I will talk to you later. Bye." I hang up, and I am not even sorry for it. She can fume at it for months.

Now why is this bloody exhaust fan not working?

Guruji arrives. He has two disciples with him. Papa is escorting him along with one of his disciples.

He is very old, around ninety-four years old. He doesn't go to anyone's house. He looks so frail now. I am seeing him after a decade. I was a little girl when we used to visit his ashram. After growing up, bhaiya and I refused to spend our vacations at his ashram, and it was hellishly difficult to convince Papa. But somehow, bhaiya did. And, Papa started spending his holidays at Guruji's ashram alone.

Papa has served him a lot. Guruji's ashram lies along the route of the Amarnath pilgrimage. Today, he has come from Jammu to Delhi, especially for us.

Papa has tears in his eyes. He is very emotionally attached to Guruji, a relation I can never understand. He says that it was Guruji who was there to guide him through his life. Guruji had told him to marry mummy, he had advised Papa to apply for his current job, which led to him now occupying a good post.

But I don't believe in all this. It is all about our efforts. If we put effort into something, then we get rewarded for it one day.

Mummy places a huge *thali* on the table for Guruji. All the items I prepared have now been showily arranged on the table. And papa has personally supervised everything. I hope the dishes are fine. Otherwise, Papa will feel hurt.

Guruji sips lukewarm water from his earthenware glass.

By the way, I am rather excited by his arrival, because I know why Papa has requested him to come home. Papa will show him mine and Neeraj bhaiya's *kundali*, the horoscope.

"Naina," Mummy says, "go bring the other dishes from the kitchen. Bring the items in the terra-cotta utensils for Guruji." She directs me authoritatively. I give her a nod, and amble to the kitchen.

I set all the ceramic plates carefully on the centre table before Guruji. I can feel everyone's eyes on me.

I stand behind Mom when I'm finished. Papa is sitting on the floor next to Guruji's feet, kneading his calves. And Guruji is patting Papa's back. What kind of a relation this is, I will never understand.

They all start talking. I sit quietly behind mom on the carpet. Papa begins introducing us to Guruji. He already knows us, of course, but given his old age, he may need this re-introduction.

Papa begins lauding about our qualifications, work and attributes.

After crowing about the feats of bhaiya, Papa now comes to me. I am feeling really nervous, but manage to flash a gentle smile to Guruji, and nod a little, to show him respect.

"Guruji, she is doing her MBA in the best college of Delhi. Many people don't even get admission into her college. Her studies are almost finished. So now, you have to help me find a perfect groom for her."

Is that all? About bhaiya, he even mentioned that he plays badminton with his friends. Why does everything about a girl begin and end with her marriage?

Guruji rubbernecks at me. I can't lift my eyes to meet his face, but I can feel his tiny, little eyes on me.

"She is doing everything you advised. She has been keeping the Monday fasts to impress Lord Shiva for six years. She is very religious, and a homely girl. She has cooked all the food today, especially for you."

Papa is elated right now, but in my head I'm thinking: please stop. I am not a homely girl. You want me to be homely, and to get me married as soon as possible. What I want is to live my life according to my own terms.

"I remember her kundali. There were a few flaws in it. And they were impactful. I don't remember much. Show me her kundali again. If she had impressed Lord Shiva with her love and dedication, those flaws and difficulties would have vanished." He speaks in a mellow tone, taking a long time to complete a sentence.

And I didn't know that he had ever said I have flaws in my kundali. Our parents are so secretive and manipulative.

Mummy quickly brings my kundali, placing it on the centre table, beside the dishes.

Guruji has not touched the food yet. Forget touching the food, I haven't seen him smile upon seeing the food either, unlike his attendants, who have been constantly staring at the plates since I set them out.

Papa opens my kundali, and shows it to Guruji. He begins examining it. My heart is in my mouth.

Guruji harrumphs abruptly. He takes my kundali from Papa's hands, placing it on his lap. He is moving his finger on some page.

I am on the edge of my seat now. He looks at me.

"Show me your hands." Okay! He throws a long glance at my palms.

"Relax your hands; don't stiffen them," he says. My heart is still thumping, and it's making my body tremble.

"Do you have faith in Lord Shiva? You keep Monday fasts for him, right?" he asks me very softly.

What do I say? Yes, I believe in god, and especially in Lord Shiva. I have fasted for him with all my heart. And whatever I have wished from him, he has granted me up till now. I don't know whether all of this is because of my fasts and devotion towards him, or if I am just overthinking.

"Yes, I have complete faith in him," I answer meekly. "And I have always prayed with an honest heart to him." He gesticulates to me to withdraw my hands.

Papa starts speaking, "Yes. She is a very sincere and cultured girl. Whatever she does—" Guruji lifts up his left hand gesturing to him to remain quiet.

"I can see in your hands and kundali. Your life is filled with trouble and danger. It is not an easy life. You have worshipped the lord with your whole heart and love. His blessings will help you in this birth, and may stop the sufferings of your soul. The person you loved the most was snatched away from you. Lord Shiva will guide you to protect yourself and your love this time. Your lover in the previous birth worshipped Lord Shiva with ardent devotion. So, he was granted his wish to marry you in this birth. You will marry your lover from the previous birth."

I am stunned. My heart is pounding like it's going to explode. I am filled with numerous emotions. I want to jump. I want to dance and shout a raucous scream. I'll marry my lover from the previous birth! Oh my god! I want to cry. My lover worshipped Lord Shiva, to marry me in this birth. I can't believe my destiny. Who can be this lucky, to marry their love from the previous birth?

"Will she have a love marriage?" My mom pries.

"It will be an arranged marriage," Guruji replies softly. His words shake me like a leaf. What? I gawp at him like a dork.

"But her husband," he continues throatily, "will be her lover from the previous birth." He starts coughing.

I don't think he will be able to talk anymore. I retreat to the kitchen immediately, to bring lukewarm water for him.

Guruji's attendant takes the tumbler from my hand and mixes some powder into it, stirring it vigorously. Guruji sips it, slowly.

Papa and Guruji's attendants take him to my parents' room to rest. In the meantime, his attendants will have their meal and rest awhile. In the evening, the session will continue.

I go to the kitchen to help Mummy.

"You start making the preparations for dinner," she instructs me, as she heads toward the living room. "I am decorating the temple. In the evening, first Guruji will do *pooja*, and then he will eat something," she says.

But my mind is full of what Guruji said. I didn't have faith in him earlier. I'd never believed him and his foretelling. I have never liked Papa serving him beyond a reasonable limit. But now I want to believe each and every word Guruji has said. I want his prophecy to come true.

Ahhh! How we get trapped in the web of our own words and perceptions sometimes. I am the one who had opposed Guruji the most in our family. I have complained and nagged endlessly about Papa's devotion to him. I never liked Papa following Guruji, because somewhere I always felt that my life was controlled by Guruji and his decisions.

But now, I don't know. Should I believe his words? Honestly, I want to believe him now. I felt different in his presence today.

Papa has never given him gems, gold or money. Papa has only served him wholeheartedly in his ashram. And see, he has come to our place in spite of many riches.

I'm kneading the wheat dough, but my mind is untiringly trying to convince me that all that the old man has said will happen!

3

"What, dude, I can't believe it. Seriously, he said all that, word by word?!" Tanvi bellows.

"Yeah! I am dead shocked since then myself!" I shout.

"What else did he say? Why didn't you call us to your house? We would have also shown him our kundalis," Ruby butts in, in her swanky way. Even her accent is different from ours. Honestly, she doesn't belong to our group.

"Do you also have a kundali, Miss Beauty?" Tanvi teasingly asks Ruby.

"I don't think so. My family doesn't believe in all this. Does he also read palms?" Ruby beams.

Tanvi face-palms, and turns to me. "Leave her. Tell me, what else did he say?"

"I didn't get a chance to ask him anything else. After that, everybody hijacked him. Papa asked him about bhaiya, and then they started discussing our financial problems. Guruji suggested a few things to resolve them. By then, it was time for him to leave. And nobody gave a f*ck about what he'd said about me. I even wondered after Guruji had left, whether he had said all those things, or had I just imagined them? Everyone was normal. Nobody talked to me about it or discussed it among themselves," I say crestfallen. Why is my family so inconsiderate towards me?

"Oh, my baby! You're a lucky girl!" Tanvi hugs me from the back.

"How can we say that now?" asks Ruby. "That she is lucky? Her previous birth would have been a century back. We don't know how her lover looks now. Is he even well-educated? What does he do? And what is his family background? We don't know if things will come up roses for her in the end." She makes a fair point.

"Woohoo! Bimbo. I can't believe it. Have you started eating an almond tree for your breakfast?" Tanvi twits at Ruby.

Ruby hits Tanvi's sneakers with her pointed heel.

"No. Please," I say, "don't take away my beautiful dream from me. I didn't even sleep last night thinking about how he would look. Will he recognise me? Will we remember our past when we finally meet each other?" I am living in a beautiful fantasy right now, and I don't want anyone to come along and pop my bubble. It is the most interesting and exciting thing that has ever happened with me up till now.

"Oh! You girls are fools." Tiger comes in with our coffees, patties and pastries. He sets the items down on the middle step, and we pick up our cups.

"Are you mad, Naina? I least expected this from you," he grumbles.

Huh?

"What did I do?" I ask in astonishment.

"I thought you were the most sensible person among all of us. And now you are behaving like a fool."

"Hey! What happened to you, bro? Are you hopped-up?" Tanvi stands, pulling him towards her.

"What did I do to make you say this to me, meanie?"

"Tanvi, cut it out!" He shows his left hand to Tanvi in defiance, and proceeds with his point.

"It is about your life," he says, looking back at me. "College is going to be over soon. And we all know that her parents will get her hitched in a year." He rambles on, while moving like a pendulum. His words are slashing my heart.

"I do not want her to corrupt her mind with such nonsensical thoughts. Her parents will not even take her approval, before fixing her marriage. She will weave many dreams now, because of that phony baba, and when none of his predictions come true, her heart will break. It will get difficult for her to accept her fatuous, ugly husband, who her family would have routed out for her."

He rests his case and waits for our opinion. Nobody speaks a word. I don't know about the others, but I am stuck at the point where he said that my parents would not even take my approval for my future husband. I'll be tied to a man I may not even like for my entire life.

"Oh shit! I didn't give it such deep thought," Tanvi murmurs.

"But why are we getting so negative? At least give it a fifty percent chance of happening," Tanvi says in her childish tone, standing up.

"Wait. Did you say that he, your Guruji, said it is going to be an arranged marriage?" Ruby asks me. I don't have words. My throat has dried out.

Tanvi bows and holds my hands, hitting her head gently with mine. "It will be all okay in the end. At least, you have a fifty percent chance of meeting your century-old lover, which none of us do," Tanvi croons.

I give a deep sigh, and her words calm me a bit. I can't do anything to change my family. They are going to do what they want. All I can do is pray to god that nothing wrong happens with me. I have genuinely worshipped Lord Shiva with all my heart. He cannot let my family ruin my life.

"Chuck it, guys," Ruby interjects. "We don't know what is going to happen tomorrow. Let's not get so pessimistic. It will all be good. It will be amazing. We will get the one who is best for us." Ruby lightens up the situation, and the three of us get cuddly. Tiger goes back to being normal too.

As we eat our cold patties, Ruby suggests going to a new bar. She had just gone there with her cousins, the night before last.

"But I didn't carry a dress with me today." I didn't even put on proper make-up this morning, I was so excited to meet and tell them the entire story.

"Yechh! It is the best idea. Today, I am going to break the dance floor. Everybody will be in awe to see my sexy moves!" Tanvi shakes her body as if a current is passing through her.

"Sure," Ruby twits. "If you are going to behave like this, then everybody will be absolutely in awe of you."

Tanvi looks at Ruby and starts jerking her body fiercely.

We decide to go to Ruby's house first. There, we'd dress in her super classy clothes. Tanvi has sworn that she will be on her best behaviour at the bar. Ruby made her swear on her favourite wine.

Ruby's house is opulent. It is like a five-star hotel. Of course it would be, because her father's family runs a famous interior designing company. Maybe they are builders too. I don't know much. Tanvi is no less. Her family is also wealthy; her mom is a fashion designer, and she has her brand and five stores in Delhi. Once Tanvi is finished with her MBA, she is going to help her mom expand her business into other states. They have already started planning their next store in Pune.

I get a little nervous when I come to Ruby's place. I feel like I don't deserve to be there, in such a big and sumptuous house. I feel much more comfortable at Tanvi's. She lives in a beautiful apartment but it's not this extravagant.

Ruby opens her wardrobe for us to pick and choose from. This isn't the first time I am borrowing her stuff. Usually, Tanvi gets me beautiful, traditional dresses that I can wear for a function and then return to her. Whenever there is a sale coming up, she lets me know, and I buy from her store. I can't afford her brand without a considerable discount. It felt terrible at first, when she offered me her clothes for Bhavya's marriage, but her warm nature made it feel like a regular thing between friends. Between the both of them, they never let me feel that I come from a less well-off family.

Tanvi is helping Tiger to wear Ruby's padded bra, much to her irritation. I get teary. I can't stand the thought of not meeting with them regularly. When we're together, I forget about all my sorrows, and life seems perfect. Will all this end in a month?

"Shuuuutt the f*******k up!" Ruby yells. My train of thoughts is broken by her outburst. I need to intervene now, before they end up in a serious tiff. I switch off the TV, take Tanvi off the bed, and snatch all of Ruby's stuff back from Tiger.

"Both of you stop it!" I say seriously.

They sit like obedient kids beside each other on the edge of the bed. I turn around with Ruby to look for party clothes. I let her pick for both Tanvi and me. I don't want to choose a dress that Ruby might not want us to.

She gives me a hot pink body-fit dress. It is absolutely chic, and I go to her washroom immediately. When I emerge, Tiger is gone. I see Ruby and Tanvi quietly applying make-up. I join them. Ruby gives us matching clutches as well.

Ruby and my shoe size is exactly the same. Ruby gets her mom's pumps for Tanvi, which fit her perfectly.

The three of us check ourselves out in the mirror; we look like divas from KJo's movies!

I am surprised to see Tanvi. She has that uber-stylish-damsel hidden inside her. Now, she is looking like her mother's daughter.

Tiger enters in a blazer. My jaw drops!

I look at Ruby. What did she do to these dorks?

"Whose is this?" I ask, touching the fabric of the blazer. Great ensemble.

"That's Vishal's!" Ruby exclaims. Oh, I could've guessed. Vishal is Ruby's younger brother. Ruby gives Tiger Vishal's exquisite watch to wear for today.

"No. I can't take it," Tiger refuses, closing the box and tossing it onto her bed.

"Heyi, it is just for today. He won't mind," Ruby insists.

"No means no. That's too expensive and too personal. I only wore this because, otherwise, I wouldn't be allowed entry to the bar." Tiger makes his point. He is looking hot. I had never thought he could look this handsome.

We all leave for the bar in Ruby's car, and on the ride over, I make a call to Mummy. I try to convince her to allow me to stay out until 7:30 in the evening. I tell her I have classes till three, and then I have to go to Tanvi's store to help her mom. She agrees. I knew the 'Tanvi's mom' card would work, as her mom had provided us with great discounts on our clothes for Bhavya's wedding.

We finally reach our destination. At the gate, Ruby asks for a table for four. It's 3:30 in the afternoon; the bar will be empty. We enter.

This place is for rich people, not for people like Tiger and me. He and I exchange a look as we go in. Only we know that today's evening is going to be very expensive for no reason.

We sit down and order our drinks, along with some snacks. We ask Tanvi to go slow. Today, we have enough time. And I have a hunch that today's an evening that I am going to always remember.

There's a singer up on stage singing romantic evergreen songs. His voice is magical. Intoxicating! There are very few people. And the lights are so dim that one can hardly make out if someone is sitting at the next table.

I'm waiting for a Red Sangria, and my head is dancing. My buzz is getting stronger with each inhalation of shisha. I rest my back on the couch. My eyes are closed, and my heart is throbbing. I am completely relaxed. We all are.

At 5:30, Tanvi gets up to dance. More people have poured in by this time. Ruby was right about this place. It's incredible, with the perfect ambience. I hate those places that have huge lights blinding you. You feel like you're being watched. But in here, it is private. I feel liberated. We move to the dance floor.

A band has now replaced the sweet boy from earlier. It is time to shake our booty! We dance like it is the last day on earth. I'm estatic with my hair flowing in the air, the cool breeze drying my sweaty back.

I make my way back to the table and take quick sips of my next round of Sangria, and it immediately begins to take effect. Bracing, I sit down and look around the room. The pub has gotten crowded. When did so many people pour in? Had I been dancing in front of so many people?

I finish my wine and inhale shisha. The music and beats are dancing in my head. The flavour of shisha wipes the bitter taste of wine from my tongue, leaving my mouth full of smoke. I get up to go back to the dance floor, but then fall back instantly. Shit! I clearly had too much.

I try again to stand first, and then, take a few mini-steps forward. I can walk – or, well, I am rocking, actually. I look for my friends. They have gotten lost in the crowd. Shit! So many people are up, bouncing like monkeys. But where are my monkeys? I don't know how to get past this crowd. My monkeys would be somewhere in the centre.

Someone shoves me. My clutch drops. I can't see the floor clearly. Somebody, please, lower the music. I can't focus. Shit! It was Ruby's.

"Hey, are you okay?" I hear a voice, and my heart misses a beat.

He holds me from the back. I feel his warm hands over my shoulder. He makes me move. Who is he? His touch electrifies my body. I can feel the heavy pulsation of my heart. Where is he taking me? He escorts me to the bar. I look at his bright face. These shitty, blinding lights make my eyes watery, but I can see that he is grinning. He has small eyes, pink lips and a lean face. He is staring at me. Shit! He's staring because I am rubbernecking at his face like a goof.

He gives me a tumbler of water, and gestures to me to drink it. I take a long sip. I was damn thirsty. He turns a bar chair for me to perch on as he hands me my clutch. Oh shit!

"Thank you," I choke out.

"What?" He brings his ear near to my face. He smells rich. I don't say anything. I can't understand anything.

He withdraws his head, a curious look on his face.

"Are you fine?" he asks softly. His voice... I think I have heard this voice in my head before.

"Yes," I say quickly.

He smiles.

"I am Raghav." He brings his hand forward for a handshake.

"I am Naina." His hand is warm.

He is still looking very curiously at me.

4

I look into his eyes. He licks his lips, then turns to the bartender and asks for water. I am sitting like a thicko on the bar chair. I get up, and he turns around to face me.

"Are you okay now?" he asks with a very considerate look.

"Yeah, I am better," I say sheepishly, tucking my fringe behind my right ear. "I drank too much, I guess."

"Did you come here with friends?" he asks, taking a sip of his drink.

"Yeah, they would be here..." I look for them in the crowd. I still can't spot them. I take my phone out of Ruby's clutch.

Shit! It's seven o'clock. We need to leave right now. I've got two missed calls from Tanvi, and a third from Ruby. Hastily, I dial Ruby. He is totally checking me out, and enjoying his drink.

Ruby, please pick up. I look back at him. He is thinking of something. He steps forward and murmurs, "All okay?"

"Yeah." I flash a big smile.

He sits next to me. Is he alone? I don't have the guts to ask him that. He is already behaving weirdly.

I try Tanvi's number now. What would he be thinking? Am I looking hot? Yeah, I am hot. There is no doubt about it. But does he think I'm hot? He is so hot himself.

God! These girls. None of them are picking up.

"Heyi!" Tiger finally finds me. "What are you doing here? We all got worried."

"I got lost. I tried to look for you guys, but see the crowd?" I say sheepishly.

Finally, I get Tanvi's call back. I bridle at her, "Where are you?"

"Where am I?" she squawks back worriedly. "Where are you, loser? We are all freaking out here. Tried your phone a million times. Now, Tiger has gone to look for you."

"I am with him now," I say cowedly. "Come to the bar counter."

I look at Tiger with a sigh of relief, and find Raghav still rubbernecking at me. *Is he all alone?*

I see Ruby and Tanvi coming towards us. Ruby notices Raghav first, and then looks at me.

Tanvi gives me a horrible look. I mutter 'sorry' to her.

"What are you doing here?" Ruby enquires questioningly.

Raghav interjects. "Hey, I am Raghav." He shakes hands with Ruby first, then with Tanvi. Ruby gets ecstatic, and Tanvi is taken aback, just like me. She and I exchange a 'who-is-he' look.

"Sorry I brought your friend here. She seemed pretty lost to me, so I just wanted to make sure that she was fine." Raghav explains.

"Wow! So sweet of you," exclaims Ruby in her svelte tone.

"Actually, it's my friend's bar. So, I prefer to make sure everyone is safe and comfortable here." Raghav sets his glass back down on the counter. This bar is his friend's? I was so right about him.

Tanvi thrusts out her lower lip in confusion. Raghav notices her expression.

"You girls can be my guests for the day," Raghav offers.

"Is this your usual thing, to invite people for free drinks?" Tanvi ripostes, instantly.

Raghav appears slightly disconcerted by her straight quip. "No," he says, "only on some special days like today. Whenever I feel a little off, I like to interact with new people. Is there something wrong about knowing other people?" He looks straight at Tanvi. God! These two can have a face-off.

"C'mon, Tanu. It is just a few drinks," Ruby pleads.

"No. It is fifteen past seven. We need to leave right now," I grouse, showing them my watch.

"Hey, it's just 7:15. And you guys want to sneak out? This is the time when people actually sneak in." Raghav lifts a glass of whiskey from the counter. I didn't see him asking the bartender to give him another round.

"She is right," Tiger insists, backing me. "Let's leave. I'm feeling a little uneasy in here. This place is getting thronged." I smile at him.

"This is how real clubs are," posits Raghav. "If you guys are into clubbing." I haven"t seen Raghav acknowledge Tiger even once. So rude.

"Yeah, we know what clubs are like," Tanvi retorts with a fake smile.

"C'mon, guys! Please, don't be party-poopers!" entreats Ruby.

What to do now? I really can't wait any longer. My parents will throw me out of their home. And Tanvi and Tiger are clearly not liking the newcomer's company.

I grab Ruby's hand and take her over to a corner.

"You know, it is late for me," I tell her.

"Darling, I know. But I am having such a good time. And he seems like a pretty nice guy."

I give her a look.

"Okay," she says. "Just half an hour. We will tell your mom that we got stuck in traffic. She knows how jammed the roads are at this hour." Ruby is not ready to give in. If I don't surrender, she will get mad at us. She'd gotten all of us ready so chicly, today.

I relent. "Okay, but no more than thirty minutes. And you will have to fly me back home in twenty minutes then, I don't know how." I am scared as hell. Mummy will be furious.

My phone rings. And it's Mummy.

"Ruby!" I scream after her. She picks up my phone and very smartly starts making excuses, detailing how we all started to eat at Tanvi's mom's store, and that now we are about to leave. She promises that I'll be home by 8:15.

Ending the call, we make our way back to the bar counter. None of them are talking to each other. Tiger and Tanvi are giving Raghav the cold shoulder.

"Okay," Ruby says, approaching Raghav, "we can stay for half an hour. Naina can't stay out till late." Tanvi looks at me, dumbstruck. I try to convince her. Raghav notices us.

He takes us to a table in the corner, where the music is not that loud. We all perch there, one by one. Tanvi, Tiger and I sit on the couch, while Ruby and Raghav take the chairs opposite to us. A waiter appears at our table immediately.

"So, girls, what are your favourites?" Raghav asks us buoyantly. This is the first time he has shown this much excitement up till now.

"I'll go for a Cosmopolitan!" Ruby beams.

"I don't want a drink," I say, looking at Ruby. "I have to be sober now, as I'll be home in an hour – hopefully."

"Yeah, you will be," Ruby drones back.

"What a spoilsport!" comments Raghav.

"Right, no?" Ruby adds, gazing at him encouragingly. She swapped sides so quickly.

"And you? I guess you will enjoy a Macallan Fine Oak 21 with me?" Raghav suggests to Tanvi. I gape in astonishment. He is daring her. He doesn't know how fierce she is.

"Why do you think so?" Tanvi shoots back instantly. She is in a snit now.

"Wait. You will know. And in case you don't enjoy your drink, I am here! The drinks will be on me tomorrow as well."

How rich is he? And how idle? Is he free all the time to offer drinks to people?

"If you have so much cash to wonton, you can give it to me! I'll be happier to have your cash than drinks," Tanvi chuckles.

Raghav guffaws. "You are a tough girl," he says to Tanvi.

Nobody asks Tiger, so I do. He shakes his head.

"So, how exciting are your lives, girls?" Raghav continues.

"We are all MBA students," Ruby answers. "The college course will end in a month. Then we all will fly in different directions, only to come back to our hive in the end."

Our drinks arrive – actually, theirs – poured into very exquisite whiskey tumblers, which I suspect they do not serve to the masses. Raghav pours me some water, to cheer with them. He has a charismatic aura, and I think he is gradually winning over Tanvi, too.

"This is nice," he says. "You guys are reminding me of my college days. I have just returned from Cornell University." He takes a small sip of his drink.

Two waiters come by, laden with big trays full of items. Who is going to eat all this?! We have twenty minutes left now. I can't sit here for any longer than that.

"No, none of us is going to eat all this!" Ruby exclaims.

"It's okay. You can at least taste a bit of every nosh." He picks up a fork and takes in a mouthful. "Delish!"

"You went to Cornell? You don't look like the swot-type," Tanvi twits at Raghav.

"And you are tomboyish," he says, "but not looking like one right now. Rather, you are looking bonny to me." He bends forward and flashes a grin to Tanvi. Ruby and I look at each other in a daze.

"I am not tomboyish! It's just that I am not gullible like other scatterbrains," Tanvi retorts, looking over at Ruby. "Also, do tomboys not look bonny to you?" She turns her eyes back to directly meet Raghav's.

"Not bonny. They look red-hot to me!" Raghav grins and swigs his drink, only to replenish his glass again.

I see Tanvi there, clearly thinking hard and ruminating on an excellent comeback. Shit! He's made her speechless. He is good. I look at Ruby and we both chortle quietly.

"Please," he raises a tray of barbeque chicken wings tossed in chilly garlic sauce, offering it to Tanvi. I know it is her favourite. Anything seasoned in chilly garlic sauce is her favourite. Out of all the items here, he's picked this one for Tanvi. How did he know that she would at least taste this one?

Tanvi thinks for a moment, and then picks up a piece with her fork.

"Why are you feeling low today?" Ruby asks Raghav.

"Not anymore," Raghav replies, giving her a winsome smile, then looks at me. I look down. One guy, trying to charm three girls at a time. Wow! He is a Casanova.

We all chat for another ten minutes, during which I find him staring at me multiple times, while still paying full attention to Tanvi and Ruby. While talking, Raghav shares his business card with Ruby, and she gives her contact number to him.

Finally, we get up to leave. Ruby and Raghav hug, and he exchanges a handshake with Tanvi. Making his way over, he brings his hand out towards me for a casual handshake. But his eyes look at me searchingly. He holds my hand longer than he held Tanvi's. I withdraw my hand with a sweet smile. He smiles flirtatiously at me.

Tiger has already gone out. We move out and follow his lead, while Ruby is still inside talking to Raghav. I spot Tiger outside, standing like a model beside Ruby's car. I go and stand with him.

Ruby hugs Raghav once again, before leaving him there.

We get into her car, and I take a seat in the back. I have to change on the way home.

Ruby gets in too. "Wasn't he so sexy?" Ruby begins.

"Only to you," Tanvi tells her immediately.

"He was wearing Roger Dubuis!" Ruby exclaims. She is completely in awe of him.

"What is that?" I ask innocently.

"That's a Swiss watch brand. His watch would be worth at least fifty lakhs in Indian currency."

"So? Why are you calculating the cost of his accessories?" I ask her.

"Dudes, seriously! None of you is smitten by this person?" she asks while driving.

"Stop it. Just because he was rich? What about his manners?" Tiger finally speaks up.

"What about his manners?" Ruby asks Tiger, agitated.

"Chuck it. If you didn't even notice it, there is no point in telling you. Just drop me off. Bring my clothes tomorrow, and I'll bring yours." Tiger is hurt, no doubt. Anyone would be.

"What is happening to you guys?" Ruby asks. "I liked him. What am I missing here?"

"Sense," Tanvi utters tersely. Ruby looks at her from her rearview mirror, but Tanvi doesn't give a damn.

"Okay," Ruby mutters.

5

I enter my house, quaking in my boots. Papa is not home, thank god. Mummy is laying out dinner on the dining table. She looks at me quietly. I don't look at her. I don't want to make eye contact. I also don't want to indulge in any conversation with her; what if she smells the booze? I go to my room straight away and lock the door behind me.

After freshening up, I come out. I tell her fake stories about Tanvi's store. She doesn't show much interest. I know she is mad at me for coming home late. But how do I make her understand? My time at college is ending. These are my last days with my friends.

I drift back to my room in some time, after flicking through the TV channels. As soon as I enter, the image of Raghav looms in my head. His mysterious smile, his curious eyes, the way he was sneakily checking me out and searching for something in my face. What was up with that guy?

I lie prostrate in bed, rocking my half legs back and forth. I can't take him off of my mind. I think, somewhere, I enjoyed him looking at me like that. His eyes were very mysterious. I felt like he desperately wanted to talk to me. But why? He is beyond-my-imagination rich. Why would he be interested in someone like me?

And Ruby is better than me, on any given day. I am not even his type. He looked like a model. He could have any girl. Then, why me? Why was he showing interest in me? Is he my lover, about whom Guruji prophesied?

No. I have started to weave dreams again. Stop thinking about him! It could be that I misunderstood his actions. Maybe he was just healthily flirting. And he'd spoken to everyone. The fact is he is Ruby's interest. I shouldn't even think about him, for Ruby's sake. And she is far better than me in every aspect, regardless. She has a better standard and lifestyle; her parents have class. She can think of swaying him. They can even give it a shot. I, with my parents and their orthodox mentality, can never. Also, of course, college is ending, and then I'll be caged in this house. There is no point in thinking of him, or of any other guy, now.

I get depressed. I've never had a boyfriend, never felt that way. Sometimes I feel like I have sacrificed a lot because of my family. Yeah, not having a boyfriend due to the fear of one's family is a sacrifice. In today's time, everyone has had at least one relationship. But not me. I have never had one. I feel that emptiness creeping up inside me. Getting married is different, and sneakily meeting with someone is different. I feel very lonely on some nights. And now, I'll be betrothed to someone, whether I like him or not. Who wants to live such a life? What is the point in living a life in which you cannot do anything according to your own wishes?

My phone rings.

It's Ruby.

"I have been talking to him," she shoots. "He sent me a message first." I don't need to ask who. And this is a bad time to talk to her about her f**king amazing life. A life I've never had, and never will.

"He seems interested in you," Ruby says casually. But what!?

"What?"

"Yes," she affirms, "he told me that he was awestruck to see you. He has been looking for a girl just like you. He liked your everything – your hair, your body, smile, fragrance, dress, the way you spoke, and so on. He has been rambling on and on about you."

My heart throbs fiercely. I get goosebumps. I don't want her to stop. He is interested in me. Me!

"I gave him your number. He will text you," Ruby drones. She sounds crestfallen.

"What? Why did you give my number? What if he texts me now?" I squawk.

"Then, you talk to him. What is wrong with that? Did you not like him?" she asks directly. I can't say that I did brazenly to her. I also can't ask her if she is okay since he chose me over her. She had been so excited about him in the car.

"I don't know," is all I say, quietly.

"You don't meet such dudes every day, Naina. It also doesn't normally happen that they like you this much. If I were you, I would have grabbed this opportunity open-heartedly and desperately."

"Hmm."

"I am not saying all this because he is extremely rich, but because of his aura. Didn't you notice that? He is so intelligent and smart. He handled Tanvi so well. He just knew what to do, and how to do it. Such guys are very rare. We only get to see them in movies or in fairytales."

I can make out she is dejected. But still, she wants me to go ahead. She really liked him. I am feeling bad for her. But now, she genuinely wants me to go for it. She is one rare soul. I am lucky that she is my friend.

"You sure I should go for him? You know about my situation at home," I ask honestly.

"Yes. That's the main reason I want you to go for it. Because you never know what is waiting for you tomorrow. Give life a chance. Even if it doesn't end well, your parents will get you hitched soon. And if it does, life will be a fairytale," she says encouragingly.

"Okay," I manage to choke out, "if you say so. And thank you, Ruby, for everything. You truly want so much good for me. You gave me your chic clothes, pumps and clutch today. If he likes me, then all credit goes to you. Thank you."

"It's okay," she replies. "Don't be stupid. Talk to you tomorrow. And in case you talk to him, don't you dare delete his chat! I'll kill you otherwise." She tries to sound excited.

"Yeah, okay. Bye." I end the call.

I look down and find a WhatsApp message from an unknown number on my phone. It says, *Hey*.

It's him. I open his display picture. It is him. He is in Paris, looking at the Eiffel Tower from a distance. He looks insanely dashing.

Shit! He comes online. I close the app immediately. What to do now? Should I chat with him? Why is he interested in me? What is so special about me? Why am I feeling so nervous? *Just think of him as some guy, Naina.*

Tentatively, I open his chat. He's gone back offline, two minutes ago. I reply, *Hi*.

My fingers are quivering, and my heart is in my mouth.

He comes back online instantly.

What's up?

I type, *nothing special*, and then delete it. Then type again, *In bed; talking to you.*

And also thinking about me? he sends.

How could I forget how smart he is? I am scared to talk to him now. Soon, he will realise he has been wasting his time.

You wish!! I reply.

What do you think? Why have I sent you a message? he responds instantly. Doesn't he need time to think about his next message?

I take time to think of a reply and then send him this: *I don't know. How would I know what's on your mind?*

You are on my mind. I can't take you out of my mind, and it is not that I want to.

His reply increases my already-throbbing heartbeats. I read his message again and again. I imagine him saying this to me, while licking his lips and trying to read my mind.

I saw you passing by me. You went to your table and had your drink. I knew you were not fine, and would tumble. I was coming to rescue you, but somebody jostled me, and so I ended up jostling you.

This made you dote on me? I ask.

You were completely out. You couldn't walk on your own. I held you, and you let me. What I found unusually sexy was your face. The way you looked at me. You looked awful, with all your hair over your face, you couldn't understand anything, but your face had that innocence, which stopped my heart from beating. When the light fell on your face for the first time, I felt as if I had seen you before. I was sure I had seen you before. I had heard your voice, even. I tried very hard to remember, but couldn't. So, what do you think... have we met before?

What is he talking about? Is he saying all this because Ruby told him about Guruji's prophecy? No, Ruby is herself interested in him. Why would she have? So, is he being honest?

You think I am trying to woo you by these stupid old tricks? he sends. *I mean, I am being completely honest with you here. I do feel that we have met before.*

It is so weird. I call Ruby.

"Did you tell him about Guruji's foretelling?" I ask her. She sounds sleepy.

"To whom?" Shit! I woke her up.

"To Raghav," I tell her.

"No, I didn't. Why would I? What happened?" She rouses.

"I don't know. Are you sure you didn't tell him anything?" I ask her again.

"No, I didn't, Naina. What's wrong?" she asks firmly.

"Okay. I'll tell you tomorrow."

Why didn't you ask me about this at that time? I WhatsApp him.

Haha. I was so spellbound by you that I couldn't. He is acting cheesy now. Surely, he is making all this up. And all those stupid things Guruji said are f**king with my mind. Tiger was right.

I tell him I have to sleep. I have classes in the morning. He insists on me meeting him instead of going to college. Is he mad? I tell him how important college is for me right now, and that I am dozing off. I don't wait for his reply, and switch off my internet.

I feel such a relief. He is totally making all this up.

The next morning, I take my phone into the washroom with me. I switch on the net, and the first thing that pops up is a notification. He's sent me many messages.

10:58 p.m.
I loved the innocence in your face. I felt the urge, please don't take it wrong, to get close to you, to know you, to learn more about you. To touch your innocence. I just want to get into your head and read your thoughts. You captivated me today.

11:01 p.m.
Have you zonked out?

11:01 p.m.
So rude. Really!! I am disappointed.

2:14 am
I still can't stop thinking about you.
What have you done to me?
It was only our first meeting.

2:17 a.m.
I can't take your face out of my mind. That first look of your face when it shone in the light. I still think I have seen you before. We should meet. This time privately. Tell me when can I pick you up?

He is the one. He is my lover. He is the one. Definitely!

6

I show my chat with Raghav to Ruby, Tanvi and Tiger. Tanvi is angry at me for encouraging him, but Ruby doesn't see anything wrong with this. Tanvi doesn't say anything to Ruby, but frowns at me.

"Really? You want to initiate something with him. A guy like him?" Tanvi shows her displeasure.

"What is wrong with you people?" Ruby asks, disgruntled. "Stop thrusting your opinions onto her."

"Tanvi, please, calm down." I caress Tanvi's arm. "I know you didn't like him. Even I don't like him that much. But I can't stop thinking about what he said."

"Very good. You are totally f*cked up," Tiger sniggers. "He is bluffing. He is shrewder than you think he is. He knows how fascinating girls find such thoughts. All his messages are flimsy, aimed to attract you," Tiger explains his point.

"Oh, yeah!" Ruby puts in sarcastically, perching on the small wall a little away from us.

Tiger ignores her twit, and continues cogently, "What I think he is doing is that he is trying to win her over." He looks around at everyone. "And that could be because of a bet with his friends.

Maybe they saw us and thought to have some fun of their own by playing with our emotions."

"I can't believe you are suggesting that. God, really?" Ruby is miffed.

"Yeah," he says, turning directly to Ruby. "Otherwise, tell me: why is he showing so much interest in her?"

They are squabbling over him now.

"Because he liked her," she replies, emphasising her point. "She enamoured him just by her simple presence."

"And who told you this? Him?" Tanvi interjects.

"Leave it, guys. You are impossible. Do whatever you want," Ruby snaps and tootles off.

Our discussion ends in a bicker amongst ourselves.

•

Tanvi takes me home. I know she thinks I am not going to talk to him now.

He hasn't messaged me since his last message – maybe because I didn't reply to him.

I open his chat and reread his messages, and I remember all that Ruby had said to me last night. His message, that how my one look stopped his heart from beating. He felt the urge to know more about me. Yes, I could feel his desperation to talk to me.

Why so desperate to meet me? I text him.

I wait for his reply. He hasn't been online since 11:05 a.m.

But I get his response in fifteen minutes. I don't open WhatsApp. I read his message from the notification bar, so that I have time to think about my reply.

Hey, beautiful! Aren't you trying to make me desperate for you by replying to my messages late? Well, it's working.

He has the charm to make a girl feel nervous and special at the same time.

Why so interested in me? I ask him with a smile on my face.

He takes time to reply.

Didn't I express my feelings in detail to you in my previous messages? I hope you haven't deleted them without reading.

Oh! You talking about those cheesy messages?

Cheesy? Really? You're calling my feelings cheesy?

Did he get offended? I was only trying to tease him.

No, I send, *I mean, I don't know if you genuinely feel that way.*

I think you undervalue yourself a lot. I have been with many girls; a countless number of girls. But I never experienced such a feeling, this current in my body, this urge to talk to someone so strongly. You are different from the crowd. You need to know your worth!! And one more thing, I think I have seen you in my dreams – not just seen you; I have spent a lot of time with you in my dreams. I want to know you, Naina.

His message moves something inside me. I can feel my pounding heartbeats. I sit on my bed and keep my phone aside, taking deep breaths to calm myself. Nobody has ever said such things to me before. He is so fearless and confident about what he wants, and is ready to fight for it. Ruby was right; not everyone is this lucky to meet such a guy.

If he falls for me, he will be fiercely in love with me, and can fight the world to have me. What else does a girl want more than a loyal husband? And he is financially very secure. Mummy and Papa should not have any objection. They will sanction our marriage. Shit! I don't even know if he wants to marry me. What if he doesn't find me worth his affections and asks me to go away? What will I do then? How will I convince him not to leave me? I am nothing compared to him.

I am brought back from my reverie by the ringtone of my phone. It's him. I toss my phone back into my hands in trepidation. I stare at the screen, but do not pick up his call. How desperate is he? I didn't reply instantly, so he called. Would I even be able to handle such an impulsive man?

He sends a message. I read it in the notification bar.

Where are you?

I exhale. What shall I do?

I am here. Was thinking about what to do, I text him.

WHY ARE YOU THINKING SO MUCH? WHAT IS THERE TO THINK? I WANT TO MEET YOU, he sends.

Papa and Mummy are already looking for a boy for me. Would this be the right time to fall for someone?

But I want to meet him. What if he is my lover?

So, I agree to meet him tomorrow. I will not go to college. I'll leave home a little late. I'll take a cab. He offered to pick me up, but I have to change and get ready somewhere, before he sees me.

I begin digging out clothes from my cupboard in order to find the perfect attire for the date. I am already blushing.

I give up at three a.m. I have shortlisted three outfits, and done my nails.

At eight in the morning, I wake up and help Mummy a little with routine chores, and then sneak back into my room. I do a mini facial first. I am still not confident about my clothes. It's a lunch meeting in a five-star hotel. What should I wear? I finally select a fourth set of clothing. I've never worn it. I bought it with Tanvi not long ago. It is an olive green kurta, with a high frontal slit. I pair it with my super skinny light blue jeans and black cylinder block heel stilettos.

I wear a plain white kurta for now, and pack the kurta and stilettos in a polybag. I'll tell my mom that Ruby wants them.

Hoisting it onto my shoulder, I manage to leave my house on time.

I am getting dressed in a shopping centre's washroom near my college when I get a call from Raghav. I have not spoken to him over the phone yet. I pick it up this time, because I am about to meet him.

"Hello," I hear his robust voice say. It seems like I am hearing his voice for the first time now, so clearly.

"Hi," I reply nervously.

"Where are you? I can't wait to see you." There is passion in his voice, and it swirls my head a little.

"I am ready. Just about to book a cab," I say without thinking much. I have gotten into a trance all of a sudden. Maybe I am tired.

"Cab? Why? Let me pick you up. When I am at your service, why do you need a cab?" he offers very convincingly.

I surrender, and give him my location.

He arrives in his lavish car. I don't even know its name, and I am going to sit in it. I feel small. He lowers the window glass and flashes his mysterious smile. I get a proper look at his face in this bright sunlight. He has curly hair, but he keeps it short. I smile back at him anxiously.

"C'mon in," he gestures.

I sit and fasten my seat belt. I am nervous. I look at him. He seems all set and enthusiastic. I can't check him out blatantly. He wears his shades; Dolce & Gabbana. What am I doing? Why am I noticing his accessories? He is rich. But shouldn't he be with some model-like girl instead of me?

"You look beautiful", he says, with a smile on his lips. "I actually wanted to see you in Indian attire. I knew you would look ravishing."

His compliment calms me. He then asks me about my college, and how I became friends with Ruby and Tanvi. He enquires about

Tanvi's views about him, which I smartly conceal. He then asks about Papa, Mummy and Bhaiya.

When we reach the hotel, a guard appears and opens my door. The chat about my life has made me feel more comfortable with him. It feels like he wants to know me. He showed so much interest in everything.

We sit opposite to each other. He places an order for both of us, after asking for my preferences. He tells me that all his meetings take place in this hotel. Soon, the manager approaches us, greeting both Raghav and myself. Raghav indulges in a conversation with him, and I try to observe him in the meantime. He brays at something the manager said. His laughter gives me shudders. My heartbeat quickens, and I feel like I am losing myself. I think I will swoon. I quickly gulp down some water.

In time, the manager moves away and leaves us alone.

"So, where were we?" he asks. "I am sorry for making you wait. I told you I come here often." He seems not to notice my queasiness.

"I don't remember," I answer tersely. He frowns.

"I think you were going to tell me about your future plans." He fixes his eyes on me. His direct eyes on me make me uncomfortable.

"Yeah. Forget about me. Tell me something about you," I pry, looking back at him. He looks like a complete stranger to me. A person who is a total stranger, and yet I am sitting so close to him. My inner voice starts yelling in my heart that there is danger around. I am having a feeling that one has when one is unsafe. I drink some more water.

A waiter comes by with poppadum and a small tray of different sauces. Another waiter brings four slices of French bread... and Raghav begins talking.

"I don't like India," he says. "Honestly, I don't like being home. Since the time I have come here, it has been a crazy experience. My family is full of drama. But I've got to take care of dad's huge business. I am his only son to inherit all of his business. Now he has gotten old. He can't make the right decisions anymore. I feel that Indians are emotional fools." He rambles on about his family, but he soon notices my lack of interest.

"Okay, leave this. What do you think about me?"

"You are still a total stranger to me. I am trying to understand you." I give him an honest reply.

"How about a wild guess? I'll tell you if you are right or wrong," he suggests.

"I think you are a confident and determined person who knows everything. You know what you want. You even know how to get it. You are smart and observant."

"And you said I am a stranger to you! You already know me so well." He licks his lips and takes my right hand between his hands.

His touch alarms my body. It sends chills down my spine. He notices how uncomfortable it's made me, but still doesn't let go of my hand.

I give him a fake smile and pull my hand back from his grip. I keep my hands on my lap now.

"Okay..." he says, "my turn. You are very beautiful and delicate. You are one of those obedient girls who obey their parents. You are very modest, and you never want to hurt anyone. You prefer to live a simple life with your loved ones."

He speaks with stark confidence in his eyes. Our wine arrives. I thought he was a whiskey guy.

"No," I reply. "You are not a hundred percent right about me." I produce a smug smile.

He sniffles. I don't think he liked my reproach.

"I am not that obedient," I continue. "If I were, I wouldn't be here with you. And yeah, I prefer not to cause trouble for anyone, but I also don't just offer myself up on a platter to be exploited by others. I know what is good and bad for me."

He spats to show appreciation. Then asks for cheers!

Our delicious food arrives. He has ordered Italian. I serve myself, and so does he.

But my inner voice is not silenced yet. It is still asking me cogently to leave. But how can I leave like this?

He sprinkles different condiments on my dish. I think he is domineering and prefers things according to his taste. He chooses for people around him. How can anyone live with such an overpowering personality?

"How is it?" he asks me.

"It's nice." I again sham a smile.

"Do you have any zeal for art?" he asks. Wow, art! That's not my thing. But surely, it is his, Mr Richie Rich.

"No. I have no idea about art," I say sheepishly.

"It's okay. I can help you build an interest in art. In fact, I'll take you to very exotic art galleries. You will not be able to resist falling in love with the artists' creation and vision." He speaks with utter satisfaction in his tone.

So I am ductile, he thinks. I can be taught and moulded according to his taste. I don't think he and I can make a good couple.

He starts narrating his story about how he developed a fervid love for art; his favourite artists and their famous works. I am neither enjoying this bland food nor his confab.

He notices it.

"What else shall I order?" he asks.

"Nothing. I am full," I say, while gulping down a mouthful. This was my last bite.

"Dessert. Come on," he insists. Today, he is a complete gentleman if I don't act like a grumpy aunt. In fact, he was that day too, back in the pub. But there, he seemed more like a party animal. Here, he is a responsible chevalier.

I shake my head in denial. He still calls a waiter and orders a chocolate and raspberry dome. I have never heard of it.

"Ladies love it. So will you. You deserve to have every exotic thing in your closet! One needs to have the eye of a connoisseur to espy the perfect piece of fine art." He's just said something that flew right over my head. But I am not going to ask what it meant. Just a few minutes more, and then I'll be free.

Our dessert arrives. It is literally a dome of chocolate with raspberry sauce all over it.

"What are you thinking of, Naina?" he pries.

"Nothing." I am not a big fan of raspberry sauce. I loathe it. But as I taste it, this thing is still bearable, not as bad as the food. Mummy-Papa are correct – five-star hotel cuisine is pathetic. It is tasteless, and repugnantly extravagant.

"I really like you," he says softly. "I got you something, as it is our first date." My heart skips a beat.

He takes out a watch box and opens it.

"It is Swarovski. Not expensive. So, you can accept it." He smiles.

But I didn't like it. I don't know what to say. I just feel he has been trying to impress me with his lifestyle. He thinks I'll be impressed by all this, whereas I am feeling even more small and distant from him.

"I can't take it. I am sorry. You shouldn't have brought it," I tell him. He closes the box and slides it to rest by my side.

"It's a gift. Keep it."

I slide the box back to his side.

"I think I should book my cab now," I say.

"What's wrong?"

"Nothing. I had a great time. I have to go home, and I can't go in your car to my place," I tell him composedly.

"Not to your place, but somewhere nearby. And please, don't take it in the wrong way. I am sorry if you didn't like it. I have a bad habit of gifting things to my friends. I am a possessive soul, and I believe, presents keep your people attached to you. I am looking for a serious relationship here. I just wanted to show you that you matter to me," he says, more and more fervidly.

"I respect your feelings. And things take time to fall in their right place. You are moving too fast. As of now, we are still strangers! You know nothing about me, and I am also learning things about you. It is good that you are looking for a serious relationship. But I think—" I stop.

"You are taking it all wrong," he says, softening all of a sudden. "Take your time. There is no rush. You don't want to take this gift; it's okay. When you are ready, you can ask for it. It's yours in my safe custody."

7

I finally make my way back home. Raghav insisted he drops me off, but I booked a cab. I had to go to some other place and change first. This is the double life that I live.

Mummy comes to my room.

"Naina, be ready at six o'clock. We have to go to a wedding. I told you about it four days ago."

"Yeah," I reply, surprised, "but you didn't say that I have to tag along. I thought you and Papa would go." I have just gotten back; I want a nap.

"Don't be fussy," she replies authoritatively. "Papa told me to get you ready. Show me your dresses."

"What? Why?" I get up from the bed.

She opens my cupboard. Shit! I hope she doesn't see all my secret party-wear. I move to stand next to her.

I take her arm and bring her to my bed. "You sit here. I'll show you my dresses. Whose function is it? Is it necessary for me to come along? Please see, Mummy. I am hell tired," I coo.

"When are you not tired! What do you think I am? A robot? That I never get tired? Your college is ending soon. After that, I will not take any excuses. You will cook one meal a day. How will you assume your responsibilities after your marriage?"

I try so hard to be nice to her. But she is full of complaints and grudges.

"I am not getting married. I don't want to marry," I splutter angrily.

She gets up and walks to the door. "You scare me, and also disappoint me a lot," she says in my face, and leaves.

I bang the door behind her a little hard. Ahhhhhhhhhhhhhh!! I feel so much anger at times.

I take deep breaths to compose myself, and switch off the light. I turn on some music on my phone.

I start ruminating on my date with Raghav, and how he changed all of a sudden in the end. Maybe he feared that I would bolt. What is he up to? Does he really like me? Is he doing all this because of a bet? He didn't talk about any of his friends. No, I don't think he is doing all this because of a stupid bet. I got a little rude with him today. I felt small in his company. Everything about him is big and opulent. That's why I felt so insecure in his company. But why was I feeling so unsafe around him? Why was I getting the jitters?

He'd acted like a gentleman throughout the entire date, but I was impudent to him. If I tell Ruby about it, she will definitely get mad at me for behaving so brusquely. He wasn't blustering about his lifestyle; that's how his lifestyle is. He has studied abroad. He was only telling me about his interests, so that I could learn more things about him. And in return, I hadn't shown any interest in him and his life. Why did I behave like that? He even confessed about his feelings for me. He likes me, when there is, in fact, nothing to like in me.

Did he genuinely see me in his dreams? Was he telling the truth about spending time with me in his dreams? Aw! This is so romantic. I should ask him about it. No, not directly. Maybe, he meant that he had a dream about me last night. But that could just be because we had chatted so late at night.

My phone rings.

It's Raghav. Shit! I get up and switch on the light first. Why is he calling me? Why do I panic whenever I get his call? My phone stops buzzing. I see the time on the screen. It's 5:35. Shit!

I lock my door immediately. What if Mummy or Bhaiya come in and see that I haven't even started getting ready?

I can't go out to iron my dress. I'll have to wear something that's already ironed.

It is ten past six, and no one has knocked on my door... yet. I just need ten more minutes to do my hair.

I am ready; still no one has knocked on my door. Have they left without me? I open my door.

Nope. They are still here. I go to Mummy's dressing room to show her my outfit. She sees me in her mirror coming towards her, and a big smile appears on her face. She turns around jovially to greet me.

"My angel. Now you are looking like my Barbie," she says lovingly.

"Help me out," she says. "Tuck my saree from the back with this pin."

I help her. She gives me my rings, a diamond locket, and her beautiful bracelet to wear.

"I am looking like a princess!" I swing my dress in merriment.

"Naina, your phone is ringing in your room," I hear Neeraj Bhaiya say as he checks his bow tie in the mirror. Papa gives me a winsome smile. I feel so happy when my family appreciates me.

I rush to my room. Who can it be?

It's Raghav. Again.

I sit down on the bed in nervousness. Why is he calling me now? What if he keeps calling me while I am in the car with everyone?

I go to the washroom and give him a call.

"Hello," I say anxiously.

"Hello, where have you been?" he answers worriedly.

"I am at home."

"Okay. Why were you not taking my calls? Is it on purpose?" he asks. I don't have much time for chit-chat with him right now. Any time now, I may get a call to leave.

"I was busy," I say. "Actually, I am busy. I am going to some function with my family. Why were you calling, by the way?" I am in haste to hang up.

"Where are you going? Would you mind if I show up?" he asks playfully.

I know it must be a joke, but it increases my heartbeat all the same.

"No. You will not enjoy it there," I reply sheepishly.

"I want to talk to you. I feel the urge to keep talking to you, Naina. I want to know what you are doing, where you are, and if you are thinking about me." He speaks with desperation in his voice. I like it.

"Naina, hurry!" I hear Mummy scream. "Why do you have to get into the washroom at the last moment?"

"I'll talk to you later. My family is calling me," I murmur.

"Wait."

I wait for him to speak. But he takes too long.

"Bye." I hang up and flush the commode needlessly.

I put the phone into my clutch.

It felt like he wanted to say 'I love you' to me. Really? Is he mad? Why? I don't feel the same way for him yet. I can't fathom his behaviour.

I get a message. It's going to be him, I know.

6:55 p.m.

Do you miss me? Do you think about me? Please lie. In case you don't.

What shall I do with him? I didn't think he would be this clingy. I had no inkling that he could even fall for me.

I am taut; his behaviour has made me worried. We reach our destination. All four of us walk together, entering the hall. The host family is standing on the left, and all the cameramen on the right. It's a big wedding. We get pictures clicked with uncle and aunty, and then walk further in. I'll find Bhavya here, and I don't want to see her.

So many known and unknown faces. I keep walking, muttering 'Namaste' to everyone, including the ones I don't even know. When you walk with your family, this is what you do. In time, we arrive in the middle. Papa and Bhaiya move to the cohort of family gents, and Mummy to the coterie of her kitty party ladies. I amble alone towards the stalls of snacks.

I didn't want to stand with all the aunties. Their talk makes me sick. All they have to chatter about is whose kid is doing what, and if the girl has turned nubile, then when she is getting hitched.

Shit! I catch sight of Bhavya. She is standing near the chat-papdi stall. I immediately swerve to the right.

"Ouch!" I bang into a guy. My head hits his chest. He holds me by my shoulders. His hair comes over his forehead and eyes. He has very silky hair, perhaps a little long for boys. He has brown eyes and plump lips. I can't feel my heartbeats. I can't hear anything. He is looking straight at my face. I do not blink my eyes, and neither does he.

"Beta," somebody speaks. But I do not take my eyes off him, nor he off mine.

"Beta, are you fine?" a lady asks again in a melodious voice. He leaves me, and I hastily take a few steps back. An aunty is standing next to him. She holds him.

"I am fine, aunty," I say.

Embarrassment takes over me. I can't lift up my eyes to look at him again. I turn around and make a dash.

"Nainaaa!" I hear Bhavya's voice. I stop, but do not turn around. My eyes have welled up. I exhale deep breaths, and then begin to turn around slowly. She and her Bhavesh come and stand near me.

"Where are you rushing off to?" she asks me.

"Hi, Jiju," I say to her husband softly. She and I are almost the same age. She shows everybody that she loves me, but only I know how she uses her money and standard of living to patronize me.

"Are you okay? You are looking like shit," she says to me and laughs. Bhavesh smiles. I grit my teeth.

"Where is everyone?" she asks, looking behind me.

"They would be around here somewhere," I say disinterestedly.

"Oh! You are alone. Didn't find anyone to accompany you? How will you eat alone? We are here to save you. And Bhavesh never leaves my side at such functions. It is okay; you will also find a good and caring husband, just not someone as caring as Bhavesh." She grins at him, and I roll my eyes.

They take me to the *pani-puri* stall. I absolutely love pani-puri. I'll eat one or two, then I will make an excuse to disappear. Bhavya says she has already eaten some.

"Will I eat alone? Have one at least," I ask her.

"I've already had so much. We are standing here with you. Don't feel shy. It is delicious."

Whatever! I take a bowl.

A hand comes forward, right next to mine, with a bowl for pani-puri. He and I ask bhaiya for pani-puri together, unbeknownst to one another. I look at him. He is the same guy that I'd collided with earlier.

I feel nervous standing so close to him. My heart starts throbbing again. I lift my eyes up to peek at him. Shit! We meet each other's eyes, and both look away immediately. What is he doing here?

He is eating by my side. We take the pani-puris one-by-one. He asks for spicy water, and I for sweet water.

"Ahem." A lady harrumphs on his right side. We both look at her at the same time. This is the same lady from before. She gives me a smile.

I leave and re-enter the middle of the hall with Bhavya and Bhavesh. But I left my heart back at the pani-puri stall. It felt so crazily amazing to eat pani-puri with him. We didn't look at each other much, though. I want to go back and look into his eyes. I want to peek at him, and see if he does the same. He reminded me of my tuition days.

Mummy joins us, and we all get ready for the entry of the groom on the stage. But I look for that guy in the crowd. I had never had the courage, when I was younger, to give a vestige to the boy hitting on me, indicating that I like him back. Papa and Bhaiya were over-protective of me, and I feared that if I ever were to respond, they would catch me and scold me for it. So, I never did, in spite of desperately wanting to. And now, it is a very trivial thing for teens to have boyfriends and girlfriends. Even Tanvi has dated six boys in her life up till now. And I, none.

I spot him amongst the crowd. He is so tall that I can see him from here, easily, despite having so many people between us. I wish he would look over to this side for once. I wait for twenty minutes, but he doesn't.

Mummy tells me that we are leaving. Please, look at me. My heart shouts at him to turn towards me.

He turns.

He rakes his fingers through his hair, and catches sight of me in the process. I look directly at him, daringly. I want him to approach me. If he does, I will not back out. He takes a deep breath looking at me, and then looks away. But I neither turn my face away nor do I take my eyes off him. He will look at me again.

"Come, Naina. Papa is waiting for us at the gate, and Neeraj has gone to bring the car," Mummy says to me. Somewhat discontentedly, I begin to walk away with her.

While walking, I turn around once, to see if he is looking at me.

He is. He is. He is looking at me – and seeing this, I stop. I can't walk away from him. Please, I want to talk to you, my heart cries.

"Nainaaa!" Mummy shouts from the back. I turn around and start walking immediately. I know I have left my heart behind, with him. I will not be able to stop thinking about him for days. I will wish now, every day and night, to meet him again. But it is not a fairy tale. This is not a story of some princess. I am no princess.

We get into our car. As soon as I get ensconced in my seat, my heart starts aching so excruciatingly that my mouth waters. I put my hand on my chest to try and suppress my feelings.

I wipe my tears away quietly. No one ever finds out when I cry silently like this. But tonight, this pain is horrible. I don't know why I am feeling so attached to him. I didn't even talk to him. I didn't even hear his voice. We didn't exchange a single word. I don't even know his name to help me look for him on social media. There is no way for me to ever meet him again. This hurts.

I check my phone. There is a missed call from Raghav, and some texts. I open his chat.

8:55 p.m.

What are you doing? I am missing you. What have you done to me? I have never felt this way for anyone.

8:58 p.m.

I really like it when you tuck your hair behind your ear. When you get nervous when I am looking at you. I know I increase your heartbeat. I saw how you felt, when I touched your hand. It calmed my body, and I felt so relieved to hold you. But it scared you. I have no intention of fooling around with you.

8:59 p.m.

I mean, my feelings are platonic. I didn't approach you because of physical desires. I like you. Also, it would be a lie to say that I didn't even once imagine us very intimately. Please, come online and talk to me.

8

We reach home, and I still haven't replied to his messages. I left them 'seen'. If I don't reply tonight, he will go manic. I change my clothes first, relax, and then sit with my cell phone in bed.

I reread his messages, and eventually start typing, but I don't know what to say. I can't stop thinking about that other guy. When I bumped into him, everything stopped for a moment. I saw his face from so close, I felt his warm hands holding me tight, and his grasp had made me feel so secure and safe. I felt so much relief in that moment. There wasn't any fear; it felt as if that was the right place in the entire world. Like there was no safer or better place than that, for me. There was peace. I felt peaceful in his arms.

But also, I have never gotten this close to any guy in my life before. So, did it happen because of that? Am I just getting desperate to have someone in my life?

11:56 p.m.

What?

Raghav sends a text.

Shit! I realise that I had sent him a nonsensical, 'hhńń'. His chat was open, and I sent it by mistake. Now, he is online. I will have to reply. I stare at the screen.

Well, if I am truly desperate, then I should have felt the same way with Raghav. But I hadn't. This means that what I felt with that guy was different. And now I don't even know how to find him. I don't have a single available medium with which I can look for him. Whose relative was he? I can't ask my relatives directly about him. I don't even know his name.

The next morning, I don't feel like going to college. There's no motivation. Does break-up feel this way? I am feeling like I've broken up with someone. But how would I know about that feeling? I haven't had a boyfriend. I even missed out on my chance to have one.

I go to the washroom, feeling utterly blue.

I am so depressed that I don't want to go to college and talk to anyone. I still haven't told Tanvi, Ruby and Tiger about my meeting with Raghav.

I want to be alone and watch some old schmaltzy movie – full of love drama.

I cry while watching the movie. But I still watch it, crying, till the end so that I can see the happy ending.

Now, I am feeling even more depressed. I will never have such romance in my life. I burst out with emotions, get up quickly, and lock my door. I sob – at one moment, as loud as a lion's roar, and the other moment, as quiet as a mouse.

When I am finally done, I wash my face and shut down my laptop. I've overeaten, and now, I am feeling pukish.

I check my phone. Even Ruby and Tanvi didn't go today. Only Tiger went to college.

I see that there aren't any new messages from Raghav. He didn't send anything after his 'What?', because he had said a lot, and now there isn't anything more for him to say.

Now, it is my turn to say something. And I have avoided him long enough. He must be feeling horrible.

Hi, I send to him.

I wait for him to come online immediately after my text like he always does.

But this time, he doesn't. I think I've really upset him.

I am sorry for such a late response, I type, *I could not think of the right reply. I needed time to process everything. I think there is no harm in trying. We both don't know how we will be together.* I click on send. And wait for his reply.

I wonder now, what did I just send to him? Shit! How could I? Oh! It is because of that stupid movie.

I open his chat immediately to delete my message, but it's too late; he has read it already. And he is online. I close WhatsApp. How can I get involved with him? Will he cooperate with my family? Will he understand my restrictions? Will he understand that my parents are already actively looking for a groom for me? I don't even know how often I will be able to meet him. Will he tolerate all that? What if, amidst all of this, my marriage gets fixed? It will be a betrayal to him.

I am so happy to know that you are ready to give us a chance. I read his reply.

I am sorry. I said all that impetuously. We both come from different worlds. I don't think we will be able to hit it off. I send him.

He calls me. What is the matter with him?

"Hello," I say, answering the call.

"What made you think that we will not be able to hit it off?" he asks directly.

"You know the difference, right? There is a huge status difference between us," I tell him.

"Sorry, I don't see any status difference," he says. And he convinces me to say yes, right there. But still, I keep my emotions in check.

"Try to understand," I reason. "My family is very different. My parents are orthodox. After college, I'll not be allowed to go out as frequently."

"We will try to find a way. Surely, we will come up with something," he says, very confidently.

"One more thing," I speak cowedly. "My parents are planning to get me hitched soon."

I don't want to keep him in the dark.

"Oh! That's a real problem. I hope they don't have a boy in mind?" he asks. I am surprised by his calm response. Any other guy would have freaked out.

"No. They don't have anybody in mind yet. But I don't want to start with something, at such a time. Because in case we end badly, it will be hellishly difficult for me to start with another relationship immediately. And I know my parents; it is stupid to even think to make them understand. I hope you understand. I am sorry," I tell him honestly.

He doesn't say anything. I understand it is time to hang up.

"Okay. I have to go. I think Mummy is calling me." I make an excuse.

It didn't feel bad to refuse his proposal. I don't know why, but I am feeling relieved. It would have only made my life more complicated.

But at the same time, I don't want to be alone right now. I sit in the living room with Mummy and help her out with household chores.

Later at night, I see another text from Raghav. He had sent this in the evening.

I want to meet you tomorrow. Tell me where to pick you up.

So, it has not ended. He still has hope. What if we fall in love? I could introduce him to my parents. And everything would be perfect.

I tell him that I will come on my own. Tomorrow is Saturday. There is no college, Mummy knows. So I'll have to make an excuse to sneak out. He tells me the time and place to reach him.

I feel like talking to someone right now... so I call Ruby and blurt out everything. She gets hugely surprised, not because I pursued Raghav, but because of my reaction. I knew that she would compel me to continue the thing with Raghav.

Conversely, if I call Tanvi now, she will give me a hundred reasons to not pursue it. Tiger is a sane person, but he will also agree with Tanvi in this matter.

Next day, nevertheless, I get ready to meet Raghav with elaborate care.

I tell Mummy that I am going to Ruby's place. She asks me why I want to go all of a sudden. Mummy wants me to spend the weekend at home. I tell her I am going to Ruby's place to help her bake the cake for aunty. It's aunty's birthday next week, so Ruby wants to learn to bake. After making a few faces, she finally agrees. I tell her that I'll be home soon.

She tells me to take the car. I tell her that I prefer a cab, but she insists.

I don't want Raghav to see me stepping out of a Hyundai i20. Then, I think... this is me. If he is so sure about his feelings, then he shouldn't be affected by the size of my car.

I drive off. Today, I have a deep feeling of foreboding. What if Bhaiya – or worse, Papa – sees me with him? But surely no one is going to be around the place that he's chosen.

What if Raghav is hoodwinking his real intentions? But what would he get by alluring me? Sex? No, he has plenty of better options if he really wants that.

Oh! Shit, shit! I can't believe myself. How could I? I am petrified now.

Thud.

Oh no! I've banged into someone's car while swerving left. Where was my mind? I can't breathe and break out into a cold sweat.

A guy steps out of the car.

What! It's the same guy from the wedding. Really? I look closely. Yes. He is that very same guy. I think I banged hard into his Range Rover Velar. My eyes get wet. I don't have the guts to show him my hangdog face, but he comes and knocks on my window, and asks me to come out.

I get out, and he looks appalled to see me. He really doesn't look happy. I walk forward to see the damage. I have dented his car. And my car! Papa will be furious with me. I am never getting to drive, ever again. It will cost us at least ten thousand rupees to get this repaired.

I already had a feeling that today was going to be a horrible day.

"I am sorry. I am really sorry. I don't know how it happened. I was driving at a normal speed, and I was driving carefully. I am so sorry." I speak in a wobbly voice, but it does nothing to change his dour expression.

"Where were you looking? I saw you. You were lost. You didn't notice this big car coming and didn't even hit the brakes!" His voice raises, and it shakes me like a leaf.

I am staring at the dent in his car. My car is more damaged. My car's left headlight is smashed, and the bumper is dented, poorly, dented.

I try to say something.

"Why do you girls drive, if you can't keep your focus on the road? Who can't see such a big car coming? I even honked, but you didn't hear it, right?" he literally shouts.

What should I do? I feel like crying. I can't offer to pay for his car's overhaul. A lady gets out of his car now. She is that same lady I had seen with him at the wedding.

"Veerain, it is okay," she says. "Let her go."

So his name is Veerain. I don't want to meet this guy ever again in my life.

She comes closer, seeing the dent.

"Oh god, are you fine, beta?" she asks me. Her concern melts my heart. She is not angry with me, rather she is worried about me.

"I am sorry," she continues. "I hope your parents don't get mad at you. Our car is still fine, but yours will need to be overhauled." She speaks caringly, and caresses my right arm.

I am deeply touched by her; she is very affectionate.

"Mom?" that guy says to the lady.

"Give me your business card," she replies, turning to her son.

"Beta, in case it costs too much, and your parents get angry at you, contact this number. Veerain will pay for the damage."

Veerain gawps in astonishment. And I am dazzled by the kindness of this lady.

"No, aunty," I say. "It was my mistake. He is right. I was lost in my thoughts. I am sorry. I am scared that my parents will not be happy to see our car, but I can't accept any help from you. And this mistake of mine will serve as a lesson for me." My voice breaks while speaking, and I turn to Veerain.

"I am really sorry, from my heart," I say to him. His expression softens now.

"I am sorry too," he says. "I bought this car last week with my own savings, and brought Mom out today for her first drive in this car." His voice is calm now.

I apologise to them one more time. Then, we all get back into our cars to drive off.

I can't believe my destiny, I was so crestfallen yesterday that I didn't know his name or anything about him. And today, I have his contact number in my hand.

What is happening? My life has turned into a fairytale all of a sudden. How did I meet him today? I moaned a whole day, missing him and wondering, would I ever get a chance to see him again in my life? And today, I spoke to him. I heard his voice! I have his phone number in my hand.

I find Raghav's car parked outside the resort. This is weird. I park my car beside his, and glancing over, I find him sitting inside his vehicle, busy with his cell phone. I honk.

He doesn't look at me. What is he so busy with? I honk again, this time a little longer. He finally raises a glance toward me, clearly agitated. But a grin quickly appears on his lips the moment he sees me. He asks me to park my car and get into his.

"That's your car?!" he laughs with amusement, noting the damage. "Oh! I am sorry. If we get together in future, you are never getting to drive any of my cars," he says teasingly. He seems to be in a pretty good mood.

"Oh, please!" I retort. "I drive very safely. Today has been a very unlucky day for me. That's all I can say in my defence." But no, it has been the best day of my life. A dream came true so vividly. I seriously could not ask for more.

"Okay – I have called you here to make this the best day of your life. And when I am with you, bad luck wouldn't dare to come near you!" he says proudly.

I don't say anything.

"I have come up with a solution to your problem," he continues, confidently. "I have given it a lot of thought, and after much consideration, this – and only this – seemed to be the perfect solution to our problem."

That feeling I'd sensed the last time I met him, I begin to feel again. That feeling of danger around me, it all comes back to me. My throat gets dry.

"Say something," he says grinning.

"What are you talking about?" I am perplexed.

"I am going to propose to you," he replies, reddening.

My jaw drops in shock. He turns, and reaches to pick up some stuff from the back seat.

He produces a bottle of champagne with two svelte flute glasses, accompanied by a ring box. I glance at the back seat. It is cluttered with all kinds of things. There are gifts wrapped in pink ribbons, flowers, a camera, and so much other stuff.

I can't fathom anything. He is pouring us a drink.

Is he mentally sick? I have just met him. It is only my third meeting with him.

Am I getting this all wrong? I should wait for him to explain it all to me.

"I knew you would be surprised greatly," he says. "You wouldn't have thought that I'd propose to you." He holds out a champagne glass for me.

I do not take it. I am panicking. Is he a psycho?

"What? Are you kidding?" I ask him in a shock.

He stops grinning.

"Look," he says, "when your parents find a groom for you, and they want you to say yes, you will have to yield to their wishes. You'll be marrying someone you don't know, and maybe you won't even like him. Isn't it better to marry me instead? And you already know me well. We will make a wonderful couple." He guffaws. Is he high?

"Have you smoked dope?" I ask him.

"No, darling. I am saving you." He laughs buoyantly.

"I am not able to understand anything. Why are you doing me this favour? What will it give you?" Is this a prank? Is he filming us?

"You." He says that one word, and takes a sip from both of the glasses. I think this is the time when I should get out of his car.

"You are unbelievable. Please, stop it. Why did you call me here?" I am panicking.

He opens the box and takes the ring out.

"Take a look at it," he says, holding it before me. "It is an exclusive piece from my store. Nobody in the world will ever get to wear the same ring. This design is only for you because you are the most special lady in my life." He takes my hand and slides the ring onto my ring finger and closes my palm. I am appalled.

"I'll talk to your parents," he continues. "They will approve of us. They can never find a more suitable son-in-law than me. I have my money invested into every business. I am my dad's sole heir. You will never have any trouble in your life. I am super rich, and madly in love with you."

I am bewildered as to what to say or do. Is he really in love with me? He loves me so much as to marry me?

"Now, this is the time we should kiss," he speaks with a smug smile.

I give him a look.

"C'mon, let's celebrate!" he says, moving to hold my hand. "I have reserved a beautiful table for us in the resort."

His touch sends chills down my spine. I don't feel comfortable. He kisses my hand. Why am I not feeling the way I felt with that other guy? Veerain was his name. We didn't even talk to each other that night, and he was so rude to me this morning – but still, I feel something for him. Why? I can't explain it. I am just happy to have met him today. I am glad I have his number in my purse. I am hoping that maybe we will hit it off. I want to know if he feels the same way for me. I had seen a spark in his eyes, when he looked at me at the wedding that night. He felt something too.

"Stop," I say to Raghav. He gets appalled and stops the car. I doff his ring and put it back into its box.

"I need time to think about it," I hear myself say. What am I doing? In case it doesn't work out between Veerain and me, will I come back to Raghav? No. It is so wrong to keep somebody as a second option.

"I am not sure about my feelings for you. I need time," I tell him. I think this is the best reply to handle the situation for now. He wants to say so many things to me. I can it see in his eyes.

He takes my hand again and kisses it. "I have very strong feelings for you, Naina. And I don't know why I am feeling so helpless and unable to control my emotions for you. I have never felt this way for any girl before. You make me feel very protective, possessive, and mad for you. Whatever you are going to decide, let me tell you, no one can ever keep you happier and more loved than me."

He drives me back to my car. I am feeling sick.

I open the door to step out – but he holds my hand again, suddenly. My heart misses a beat. It scares the shit out of me.

I pull my hand from his grip with a smile, heading straight back to my car. I don't feel like looking back at him.

Finally, when I am ready to drive, I throw a quick glance at him to bid goodbye. He is staring right at me, intensely.

I drive off.

9

I knew Papa would get angry. Mummy scolds me a lot. She says that I am far too careless and insensitive. Papa listens, quietly, while Mummy chides me. It gets on my nerve.

"Enough!" I shout. It shocks everyone in the room. Mummy gets quiet, and Papa looks at me angrily.

"What do you want me to do?" I ask them. Mummy sits back on the couch.

"I try my best to keep you people happy," I say. "But as much I might try, sometimes I feel that you will never be satisfied with me." I speak with a broken heart.

"What have you done in your life?" Papa asks me.

My heart skips a beat. Tears begin to cascade down my cheeks.

"Whether you people count it or not, I have achieved a lot in my life. I have never embarrassed you; you have never received a single complaint about my behaviour in school; you have never had to run here and there to get me admission into a good and renowned university. I got the admission because of my calibre."

"That's all?" Mummy asks me. I look at her face. According to her, apparently all of this is nothing. She has lost all respect she had in my eyes tonight.

"That's not all. After that, I got admission into MBA, again in the best college, only because of my hard work. My grades have always been brilliant. It is not that I cannot earn money. If I were allowed to appear in interviews for the placements, I would have fetched an excellent job with a brilliant package." I finally say it.

"Enough!" Papa squawks. His voice shakes me. "We have had enough on this topic, and not for the first time. In our family, girls do not work outside like men. You are twenty-four now. It is time for your marriage. Learn cooking and other household chores from your mother. Learn to be a courteous lady like your mother. We know that you have many complaints. You think we have differentiated between our children. But if we had, you wouldn't be so well-educated today. You hold your head high today, in front of all our relatives because of manners and education we imparted to you. We have always provided you with the best that we could. I know how much your mother has covered-up for you. She does all the work on her own. You should think of assuming those responsibilities now. We have done everything for you, and you have never done anything for us in return – and now, you will be married. You will never get a chance to do anything for us after your marriage. Better do something now. You only want to wander with your friends. Your friends didn't toil day and night to give you all the privileges you have; we did."

He goes to his room, leaving me seated like a dead body on the couch. Mummy follows soon after.

"Why do you upset them so much, Naina?" Neeraj bhaiya says to me, appearing over my head. "What pleasure does it give you? What will make you happy? You have everything. Now, your studies are over – stay at home, watch TV. If you want to go out, go with Mummy to her kitty parties. This is how women live. It is a pleasure given to ladies that they don't have to sweat blood outside their home to provide a happy life for their family." Bhaiya is imparting his profound *gyaan*. But he soon leaves me to myself.

Everyone is now gone to their respective rooms. I walk to mine, dragging my stiff body and locking myself in. I do what I can do best, I cry the whole night.

The next day, I do not talk to anyone on my own; I only answer their unnecessary and unwonted questions. This is not the first time I have been subjected to such cruel and unkind behaviour.

I help Mummy with cooking and serving Papa his food, but I can't tolerate these cruel strangers anymore.

So once it's done, I head back to my room and lock the door behind me. I know my mother will come up soon, and will get furious to find my door locked from inside.

But today, nobody knocks on my door. Nobody realises that I have been crying since morning in my room. What wrong did I do? Yes, I banged the car, and it will cost us around seven to eight thousand, as per Bhaiya's estimate. But this was only my first time. Why is Mummy so full of spite for me? Why is she never happy with me?

Only because I do not work in the kitchen? She is the best cook, I agree, but your children don't need to have the same preferences and desires as you do. I love to work outside the home. I love to work on social media websites, and find different ways of promoting things. Just ask Tanvi; I have helped her so much in promoting her mummy's stores and designs. I am so good at it. I have so many great ideas for start-ups! Tiger always admires me for that. We had even formulated a plan to have our own start-up one day.

Now, all of that is going down the drain.

I am tired of explaining myself to Mummy-Papa. They don't understand, or maybe they just don't want to understand. They ask me, what wrong have they done to me? They don't let me live my life and take decisions for myself. I feel like a robot at times. Come feed instructions into me, and I will perform accordingly.

"Nainaa," I hear a voice calling. Neeraj bhaiya knocks on my door.

I wipe my tears immediately and unlock the door.

"Come, Papa is calling you," he says, very politely.

Papa is still at home? I am surprised. Oh! Today is Sunday.

They tell me that they have received a marriage proposal for me, and that the boy is very handsome. His family is very well-settled and respectable. They are not expecting us to spend much on the wedding, and instead want to offer their help for the arrangements. Mummy and Papa are ecstatic. Mummy tells me to sit down next to her.

She tells me that he is an only son, who lost his father at a tender age. His mother had seen me at the wedding we'd attended a few days back.

That wedding reminds me of Veerain. I had thought of contacting him. But now I have no time, and absolutely no energy for any more drama.

Mummy shows me the picture of the boy on her phone.

I lose my breath. It is Veerain! I shoot up from the sofa. My head gets dizzy, and I can't breathe. I swoon.

They all get panic-stricken. Mummy fetches me some water. They lay me down in bed, and Papa rubs my feet vigorously. Bhaiya checks my blood pressure. It's a little high, and I know why. Mummy gets me a sweet drink to sip.

I finally manage to sit up with the support of the back of the bed.

"I met him and his mother yesterday," I begin to explain. "They are the ones I had an accident with." They all gawk at me. I purposely used the word 'accident'.

"Accident?" Mummy repeats in a low voice. "Yesterday, you said that you bumped our car into someone's car."

"Yeah, I intentionally banged my car into theirs," I snap.

"Why do you want to bring that topic up again?" Papa says to Mummy.

"Beta, I am sorry," he continues, turning back to face me. "You know I didn't mean all that. All I want for you is to get you married into a good family. And if your in-laws allow you to work, then you can." He caresses my head. I understand that he is the father of a daughter. He fears, and hopes that nothing wrong happens with his daughter before she gets married. Do all fathers think like this?

"So, did his mother speak to you?" Mummy asks me, refocusing the conversation.

"Yes," I reply. "She was very sweet. The first thing she asked me was whether I was fine, and making sure I hadn't been injured." I speak in a taunting way to Mummy.

"This is wonderful! This means she liked you. That's why she found a relative to contact us," Papa says jubilantly.

They are all happy.

But I feel febrile. I didn't sleep the previous night, and I had cried so horribly that it made my chest ache.

10

Papa spoke with Veerain's mom over the phone yesterday. They have both decided to have a joint meeting today, directly, because according to them, Veerain and I have now met each other twice, and my family and Veerain's family have found out that they share many mutual relatives. This means I'll be meeting Veerain with his family today. His family is going to inspect me.

I have butterflies in my stomach. Earlier, it seemed very romantic to me, but now, I am a complete bundle of nerves. I even woke up at 6 a.m.

I can hear the commotion outside. Mummy, Papa and Bhaiya have been preparing for this meeting since last night. On Sunday, my family had spoken to many relatives about Veerain's family, and tried to obtain as many details about them as possible. Then, yesterday, Papa spoke with Veerain's mother and Tauji over the phone. And by nightfall, they had come to the conclusion to fix today's meeting.

I have saved Veerain's number in my phone. I open his chat on WhatsApp every ten minutes, and I have even caught him online four times till now. I can't see his display picture and status, as he doesn't have my number. But seeing him online makes me feel like he is close to me.

Is all of this really happening? I met a guy and felt attached to him immediately. I felt the pain of separation from him with every step I took away, and then a day later, he appeared once again in front of my eyes, from out of nowhere. And today, our families are contemplating our marriage. I just can't believe all this is happening!

Mummy barges in with a bundle of sarees and suits, and so... the preparation starts.

At two o'clock, my beautician arrives to get me ready. She begins with my hair.

I have searched for Veerain on Facebook, and I was actually able to look up his profile. He doesn't upload many pictures. He has very few pictures, in fact. He seems close to his mom. That's obvious. I know she is the one who has made all of this possible. She is the one who found me suitable for Veerain.

My phone rings.

It's Raghav. In horror and shock, I let it ring. I'd forgotten about him completely. I had muted his chat on the night of my argument with my parents. I didn't want to talk to anyone then, and later, I forgot to unmute his chat. It's been three days since then. How did he manage not to call me? He would probably be getting maniacal by now.

My beautician asks me who it is; who's getting so desperate to talk to me. Raghav crosses all limits; my phone won't stop ringing. Finally, I just switch it off.

Now I am regretting meeting him that day. Why did I send him those encouraging messages? But I didn't know he was so unhinged that he would propose to me. His words begin to reverberate in my head, haunting me.

Mummy comes in, handing me her phone before turning around and heading back through the door. "It is Ruby. She says it's urgent."

I immediately get it: Raghav must have called Ruby.

"Hi," I say to her.

"What have you done?! Raghav called me. He is getting mad. He wants to talk to you right now." She speaks alarmingly, and honestly scares the hell out of me.

I go to the balcony.

"I didn't do anything," I tell her. "My family is taking me to meet a guy today."

She gets hugely surprised that I didn't tell them about it. I calm her first.

"So, what will you do with Raghav now?" she asks.

"What to do with him? I told him that I don't feel the same way, and that I need time to process everything. Why doesn't he understand?" My voice breaks due to fear. I don't want Raghav to do anything stupid to spoil everything.

"He doesn't seem to understand," Ruby says. "I am getting his call now. He said he just wants to talk to you. Shall I put him on conference? You can tell him no, that you are busy, and that you will talk to him later tonight," she suggests.

I decide it is better to talk to him with Ruby rather than by myself, so I agree. She proceeds to add his call to ours.

She speaks first, and tells him that I am on conference call too.

"Why are you not taking my calls, Naina?" he begins straight away. I sense anger in his tone.

"I was busy. My family got mad at me for damaging our car. They scolded me badly. And then I got very gloomy. Today, I am busy. I am going to a function with my family." I speak haltingly. I hope no one is eavesdropping on my conversation with him.

He doesn't calm down. He is repeating the same thing again and again, saying that I am purposely trying to avoid him. He wants to meet me. He wants to talk to my parents. Is he out of his mind? My throat parches, and I feel like I'm going to go into a cardiac arrest. Ruby tries to soothe him, telling him that it is not what he thinks.

I hear Mummy's voice screaming for me. "Naina, are you out of your mind?! We have no time here." She comes into the balcony, fuming. "When will you stop throwing childish tantrums? Grow up now! At least now, when we are going to see a boy for you!" Mummy is almost ready.

I get breathless. My head spins. I hope she doesn't snatch the phone away from my hand and hear Raghav's voice.

But she leaves, and I breathe a deep sigh of relief.

"You are going to meet a boy?" Raghav speaks.

Shit! He heard it. I don't know what to say now. So, I hang up. My phone is switched off. I call Ruby. She picks up.

"Please, handle him," I implore her. She says she doesn't know how. All she can do is block his number. And I think that I should do that, too.

"Didi, it is getting late. Aunty is shouting. Please come inside," my beautician comes out to call me.

I start getting ready, and I do not switch on my phone the whole time. I am so scared. He told me that he wants to talk to my parents. Will he ask for my hand? I messed it all up.

No, I didn't. He did. He is acting like a psycho. I'll simply block his number, and will handle him after talking to Ruby and Tanvi.

We all leave for the meeting, which is being held in a five-star hotel.

I can see, Papa is a little nervous. He thinks that Veerain's family's status is too high for us. He wonders if he has done right by agreeing to meet with them. My family had never even thought of an alliance with such a high society family. My dad can afford to invest a high amount, but even then it is only one-eighth of what Veerain's family plans to spend.

Papa is right. This idea of meeting them is stupid. What were we thinking? It will never work out. Mummy is saying we must not think so contrarily at this time.

But they are too affluent for us.

"We have raised our children well," Mummy speaks reassuringly. "They should be concerned about our daughter, and not our status. Wouldn't they have tried to find out about our status before contacting us? They know about our status and capacity already. They shouldn't raise any objections now. And our daughter has grown up with the kids of their society. Ruby and Tanvi both come from wealthy families."

We reach the hotel, and it gives me the heebie-jeebies.

They haven't arrived yet. We reserve a long table. We have no idea how many people might be coming.

After some time, they arrive. My heart is in my mouth. I stay seated. I see two uncles and three ladies coming to our side. One of the ladies is Veerain's mom. I finally manage to get up, with my hands joined, and greet them all very politely.

We all settle in our seats, as all the older people start talking. I do not raise my eyes to see them. What if I make eye contact with any of them? Soon enough, Veerain also joins us. My heart starts pounding fast. He stands opposite me, then goes to touch my parents' feet and shakes hands with Bhaiya and sits next to him. Strange! I was expecting him to sit opposite me. My parents start talking to Veerain.

They are all laughing more than talking. These are all nervous laughs. But now, I am not feeling nervous. Everything seems fine. I'd been worried in the car, wondering how they would greet us. But seeing them now, they all look down-to-earth. My eyes meet with one of the two ladies I don't know. I smile at her a little shyly, and lower my eyes.

They are warm and congenial. My fears begin to dispel completely.

Unexpectedly, my phone starts buzzing in my clutch on the table. I calmly take it out.

It's an unknown number. I disconnect the call. My phone is on vibrate. Again, I get a call from the same number. It is Raghav, of course. It sends chills down my spine. I notice all the ladies looking at me. I switch off my phone, and put it back inside my clutch.

The group conversation goes on. Veerain's family asks me about my hobbies, and they do a little bit of digging into my beliefs and character. Apart from that most of the time, I am seated quietly.

"Bhaisaab, Veerain and Naina can now talk to each other alone. At last, it is their decision. Our chitchat will go on," Veerain's mom says to Veerain's Tauji, very decently.

It makes me excited and nervous at the same time. They all agree to give us some alone time.

Veerain moves behind my chair. I get up and follow him, without looking at anyone. We take a walk to find an idyllic, peaceful place to sit and talk. He keeps on walking ahead, and I spot a place near a fountain.

"Veerain," I call out his name. It sounds weird to my ears. But I am really happy to talk to him, finally.

He turns around. I gesture towards a table and chairs situated near the fountain. He begins to walk that way.

Now I'm feeling a little anxious, but in a sweet way. He sits comfortably in his chair, and I do, too. I wait for him to start the conversation. But he doesn't.

He is looking so dashing in his cream white suit. I am wearing a body-fit orange-coloured suit, with a long dupatta and big, antique earrings.

He is checking something on his phone, as a waiter brings coffee for us. I think he is avoiding me. He hasn't looked at me even once. So I take my phone out too. I know how to ignore people as well. But then, I immediately feel bad. I wanted it to work out. But he doesn't seem interested in me at all. Has he come to meet me under pressure from his family? Does he like somebody else? His mom could have forced him to come and meet me today.

I become sure that he doesn't want to marry me. He is idling away time. I switch on my phone now. I instantly get a notification of fifteen missed calls from that same unknown number. I open Raghav's chat, but my phone starts ringing again. I reflexively cut the call in trepidation, which causes Veerain to look at me. And then it strikes me – I am the girl who hit his brand new, extremely lavish car. This is why he doesn't like me.

But that day, at the wedding, I had felt that he liked me too. He looked back at me.

My phone rings again, and this time I don't cut the call. My phone is on silent, but it is flashing while ringing. Veerain notices, and it makes me feel ticklish. I am enjoying sitting so close to him. Please look at me, Veerain. I see his long and slender neck. I feel the urge to kiss him below his right ear. He sees me ogling at him.

"Why don't you pick that call?" he says to me. But I sense the sarcasm in his question. He wants me to kill time by talking on the phone.

"Yeah, that would be a better way to kill time, right?" I reply sourly. He gets it.

My phone doesn't stop ringing. My God! Raghav is demented.

"I am sorry. I shouldn't have come today. It is my fault, not yours." Veerain finally says it. And it breaks my heart. I try not to let it reflect on my face.

"Yes, it is your fault, and also very insulting to me," I say caustically.

"Look, I don't want you to feel bad about anything. You are very pretty. It is just that I don't want to marry this soon. I still have to achieve a lot in my life. I do not have time for all this. I have to expand my business. There is a lot of workload on my shoulders. Do you understand?" he says contritely, but it doesn't make me feel any better about it. I thought that my destiny had brought us together.

"Then why did you agree to meet me?" I ask.

"Because of my mom. She found you really sweet and decent," he replies cutely.

Why? Why can't he fall in love with me? Raghav had fallen in love with me for no reason! And here, he at least has a reason that his mom likes me. But still, no magic is happening. What can I do to make him change his decision?

I could ask him something like "what work pressure do you have?" Will that make me look desperate? Shit! Yes. He would think that I am trying to convince him.

"Why don't you take that call?" he says, pointing at my buzzing phone.

"It is not important," I say to him meekly.

"I think someone is in desperate need of talking to you." He grins, speaking derisively.

"Not important," I shoot back snappily.

"I guess that's your boyfriend," he scoffs. "Why are you torturing him?"

His barb pierces into my heart.

"He is not my boyfriend," I say. "I am not that type of a girl, who has a boyfriend and comes to meet a boy. I don't enjoy playing with someone's feelings."

"Okay. So, that's a 'he', at least. I was only guessing." He sniggers.

Who is he? Sherlock Holmes?

"Okay. Why is he calling you so manically?" he continues, this time inquisitively.

"I don't know what I did to make him behave like this," I answer exhaustedly.

"Yeah. Every girl says that in the end. So, you friend-zoned him?" he snickers again, but this one has a bitter edge.

"I think some girl must have ditched you really bad in the past. But I am not like that," I say back very defensively. How can he judge me like that?

"Wow! Please. Anyone would think this way. If that's some dude, he desperately wants to talk to you. It is so clear that he likes you, and you two have some history. Otherwise, why would anyone get one's self-respect bruised so savagely?" He gets excited. What does he know? This is hugely offensive and outrageously unfair.

"I am the victim here. See my phone." I get loud. I open Raghav's chat, which I have myself not read. But I am sure it will prove my innocence.

Veerain doesn't show any interest in reading it, but I still hand over my phone to him with the screen open.

"Read it. You will come to know," I say to him. He laughs, and then starts reading it.

I force myself to take a moment to breathe. I think I got over-excited. But how on earth could he blame me for Raghav's behaviour?

Veerain gets so serious while reading Raghav's messages that it scares me. I snatch my phone back to read them myself.

"How is it going, guys?" Neeraj bhaiya barges in, all of a sudden. It almost gives me a heart attack.

"Yeah, we were just coming back," replies Veerain shyly.

"It is okay if you want more time. I came to see if you guys are even talking or not. We all will wait." Bhaiya says to us and leaves. He is so merry that it makes me feel awful.

I check the time. We have been sitting here for more than an hour. Everyone must be thinking that we like each other. That it's going to be 'yes'.

"I think we should go now," Veerain says after a long pause. I nod to him.

"It was nice talking to you, Naina," he continues, speaking like a gentleman while buttoning his blazer. I know he is going to mortify me in front of everyone soon, by rejecting me.

"I wish I could say the same," I mutter, and walk off.

He chuckles in astonishment, but I don't look back.

11

We finally get back home. Everybody was so cordial and courteous in Veerain's family. I had felt, in the beginning, that his aunts weren't very happy about me, but later, they had looked more convinced.

In fact, everyone seems convinced except Veerain. Mummy and Papa have asked me several questions on our way back home about my meeting with Veerain, and I have told them that I don't know what he would say. Throughout all their interrogation, they didn't ask me once how I found him.

They truly don't see anything wrong with him. According to them, he is an epitome of a great son. Even now, they are singing praises of Veerain, of how well he takes care of his mom and their business, and how he is a responsible person, and blah, blah, blah.

I can't stand to hear any more stories about Veerain and how godlike a person he is. I feel horrible. I come to my room and shut the door behind me.

I fell in love with him the moment I met him. That's how strong his aura is. He is attentive towards his duties. No girl can resist falling in love with him.

I cry. My heart aches. Once again, I feel the same pain I did when I first met him that night.

When will their response come? Tomorrow... or maybe a day after tomorrow. Till then, can I at least dream of him as my future husband?

No. I burst out in tears. I call Tanvi, and tell her everything I can about Veerain, and how I came across him. She tells me on the basis of what she knows that I am the perfect lady for him. I tell her that she thinks so because she loves me. But she consoles me, and makes me feel strong and confident. I tell her that I want him to say 'yes'. That I liked him. And that it will break my heart if he says 'no'.

She asks me to stay positive, and starts suggesting some stupid tricks to make him say 'yes', to which I firmly say 'no'.

I feel a lot better after talking to her, and lie down to get some sleep.

However, I am quickly awakened by the buzz of my phone. I check it drowsily. It's an unknown number – again. I had blocked the previous numbers. I pick up this call, and hear the very alarming voice of Raghav. It stops my heart for a moment. I sit back in complete darkness.

"Are you okay?" I ask him in trepidation.

"Why're you doing this to me? I behaved so nicely with you. I treated you with so much respect. I cared for your feelings."

He doesn't stop. He sounds really hurt. Like I have cheated on him. Like we have been dating for a long time, and now suddenly, he comes to know that I am betraying him.

"Why are you talking like this?" I ask him sharply. "What have I done to you to make you feel this way?" My heart is pounding hard. I am scared.

"I proposed to you, Naina. I love you," he says, weeping.

Aw. He is crying. Why does he love me? What is there in me to love? How can he love me so easily? A guy like him. He seemed so robust and determined when I first met him; and today, so sensitive. So cowed and fragile.

"Say something. Was it a mistake to confess my feelings to you so soon?" he asks whiningly. I am feeling awful. I hurt him.

"I am sorry," I begin, "but I don't feel the same way for you. I could never think that a guy like you can ever fall for me. I am a simple girl. I live a very dull and boring life—"

"Oh! Please, shut up," he interrupts me. "I am not interested in your sympathetic speech." His voice grows intense and firm. I check the time; it is half-past twelve.

"I like you, Naina. And nobody can keep you more loved and happy than I can. You don't know that now, but you will realise that, when you spend some quality time with me. I feel a connection between us; you will feel that too. Are you following me?" He speaks so resolutely, it irks me.

"I'll come to meet your parents formally," he continues. "I am giving you a chance to accept my offer before that. I'll call you tomorrow."

It scares the shit out of me, and I shoot up from my bed to switch on the light. My breathing gets fast, so fast it's now a pant.

"Relax, darling. I love you. Have a good night," he says, but waits on the line for me to speak.

My mind is exploding with numerous thoughts. I don't know what to say. I hang up in rage, leaving him with no reply. I want to punch hard into the wall, to vent it all out. But I can't; it will wake everyone in the next room. How could he?

Not knowing what else to possibly do, I call Ruby. I just need somebody to talk to right now. She doesn't pick up. So I call Tanvi. She doesn't pick up either. So I call Tiger. Tiger should pick up, but he doesn't. What the heck? I throw my phone onto the bed, taking deep breaths to try and calm myself.

He knows how much I fear my parents. Shit! He's literally threatening me to agree to his proposal, or else he will involve my parents in it.

At four am, I'm taking a shower. I still can't sleep. I spend the whole night wondering about Raghav, reading his messages all over again. My head finally dozes off around 6:15 in the morning, due to pure fatigue.

Mummy wakes me up at eleven o'clock in the morning. I can't believe she let me sleep this late. But now, she hugs me. What is wrong with her? This is me, not Bhaiya.

"My baby didn't sleep well last night?" she asks very lovingly. "I heard you fidgeting last night," she continues. "Then, I thought to give you your own time. It happens before marriage. We have many different thoughts about our new home, and especially about our future husband."

Oh! she thinks that I am nervous about marriage. It reminds me that Veerain is soon going to say 'no'. Then, they will all be disappointed with me again.

"Veerain's mom called this morning," she says. "I didn't wake you up, though I badly wanted to." My stomach moves to hear this.

Mummy's eyes get teary. This makes me nervous. I feel weepy too, but control my emotions.

"Oh, you've woken up!" Bhaiya comes in, holding a box of sweets. He puts a piece of sweet into my mouth, and I grouse softly, "I haven't brushed yet."

Papa comes in too, very gleefully. I get why they are so happy.

Veerain has said 'yes'. It shakes me to the core. The sweet tastes bitter on my tongue. I am not happy.

Mummy, Papa and Bhaiya, all of them, hug me one-by-one. They start singing cheesy Bollywood songs. They are overjoyed, and I can't help but get emotional.

Mummy asks me to get ready, as the pandit ji is about to come and give us the auspicious dates for our functions.

I can't believe Veerain has agreed. Why? What is happening in my life? It looks so messed up.

When I emerge from my room I hear Mummy talking to Veerain's mom over the phone. It gives me the jitters. Bhaiya comes to me and whispers in my ear, "Do you want Veerain's number?" His voice is jubilant.

"I already have it," I say, shamming a smile.

Mummy tells us that Veerain's mom is insisting on a wedding as soon as possile, and that they are ready to provide us with their full support to arrange everything. Papa talks to Veerain's tauji on the phone. They all come to the conclusion that my family will give fifty lakhs in cash to Veerain's family, and that all the expenses and arrangements for the wedding will be done by Veerain, according to his family's predilection and taste.

All of this makes me queasy. I want to vomit and now my head is reeling.

Veerain's mom calls Mummy to tell her that their pandit ji has now given a date of one week later, for our ring ceremony to take place. Everybody agrees to this very joyously... and I run to throw up.

As I come back from the washroom, I find them all discussing about the function. Mummy tells me that the wedding date has been fixed for one month from the ring ceremony day, and that all we have to do is lots of shopping. Aside from that, just rest, and everything will be taken care of by Veerain's family.

Papa increases our budget, seeing the status of Veerain's family. They have decided to give fifty lakhs to Veerain's family in liquid. And above that, ten lakhs worth of gold, and then around five lakhs will be spent on our clothes. This is their estimation.

They are so happy. They are ready to spend their hard-earned and saved money so frivolously on my wedding. I get emotional. I have never felt so important to them before.

They love me. I am their child, and they are so happy because of me. No, because of Veerain. He said 'yes'. But why? I'll marry him without any objection now, even if he is planning to divorce me a month later.

I sit quietly and watch them all abuzz with activity. I think of Raghav. What will he do when he learns about all this? He will turn mad, and definitely do something stupid. I don't want him to interfere in my life.

I haven't returned anyone's calls all day. Ruby has tried to call me three times now. Tanvi and Tiger have also called. I go to my room, to talk to them and discuss everything. But my phone starts ringing.

It is Veerain. Oh my god! It is Veerain. How did he get my number? My fingers tremble, and my heart is in my mouth.

"Hello," I say anxiously.

"Hello. This is Veerain. Is this Naina?" He speaks formally.

"Yes," I respond curtly.

"Hi! How are you doing?"

"I am doing good," I answer. Thoughtless.

"Okay. That's good. Nice..." And then comes an awkward pause. I get it. His mom has asked him to call me.

"My mom told me that our ring ceremony has gotten fixed for next Wednesday. So, we have exactly seven days left. I'll soon get super busy with arrangements, and I do not have any helping hands here. I have to manage my business affairs as well."

He sounds perplexed. What exactly does he want to say? Has he called to make me say 'no' to this wedding, because he can't? I can't do that either. My family would kill me.

"So... so... so my mom wants me to take you to a jewellery shop tomorrow, to select your engagement ring." Oh! He is feeling shy to ask me out for tomorrow.

"Okay," I say teasingly. "I'll come – but only on one condition."

"What?" He sounds surprised to see my brazenness.

"You tell me your reason for marrying me first. Why did you say yes?" I ask forthrightly.

"Why did *you* say yes?" he ricochets my question right back at me.

"Because I genuinely came to meet a guy yesterday to get married," I reply, pouring my heart out. "And I didn't find any serious flaw in you that I could use, in order to convince my parents to deny this proposal – unlike you. You told me that you don't want to get married. So, then, why are you?"

"I am sorry for yesterday's behaviour. Yes, I had thought not to marry this early. But then, after meeting you, everything changed." He speaks indifferently.

"Explain," I say sharply.

"Everybody liked you," he says. "My mom immediately imagined you as her daughter-in-law. They all were lauding you and your family. Seeing that, it made me rethink my decision. I thought that you were not a bad deal. Tomorrow, I may not get such a good deal. So, I decided to clinch this particular deal."

"I can't believe you just said all that. It is not a business deal!" I am hugely stunned by this guy.

"This is the best I can say. And thanks for—" He stops abruptly.

"Thanks for what?" I ask.

"For considering my feelings. I didn't think that you would ask me about my changed decision." Maybe he didn't intend to hurt me. But this statement pierces straight into my heart. Am I some cheap, roadside girl, for him? That just because he is so rich, I'll blindly agree to marry him? He's forgotten that this whole marriage proposal came from his family in the first place.

"Hello, mister. Every time I talk to you, you irk me to the core. What do you think? That you are Richie Rich, so I'll have no objection in marrying you?" I burst.

"I have many options other than you," I continue. "I liked your mother, and that's why I came to meet you. And I showed you yesterday, the kind of boys who are in line to get my attention. One example is Raghav. He is dying to marry me, and he is ten times richer than you. If I wanted to marry money, I would have chosen him long before you."

"The Queen of Jhansi! Are you done? I didn't mean it in that way. Leave it. It is my bad that I said it. By the way, what did you do with that guy? Did you talk to him?" he asks, sincerely.

"Yes, I did. And he didn't take it well."

"Just block him. You don't need to talk to such guys. They get clingy right after two or three meetings. Don't try and explain things to him. It will only add more worries. Rest... we will discuss tomorrow, when we meet."

I like the way he showed concern for me. He doesn't want me to talk to any other guy. Is he jealous or concerned for me? I loved it.

"Okay. Thanks for showing concern for me – which is strange, by the way," I tease.

We end our call on a sweet note.

I can't believe I just talked to him over the phone. It always feels so easy to talk to him. We already fight like couples!

12

I start getting ready for Veerain. I am already running late. He could come by any minute now.

Mummy was telling me that my face is turning wan; that I am losing my glow. How do I tell her that I am not getting enough sleep, and explain to her the reason for my sleep-deprivation?

Also, Mummy has been extremely sweet to me, since my marriage got fixed. She has never showed as much love and care for me before.

She's tried to relieve my tension by saying that I am a perfect lady, and that I'll impress everyone after my marriage with ease. She said this to me. She! She thinks that I can cook almost everything. I can take care of the home well. She is absolutely confident that I will be a wonderful daughter-in-law. It was so much to process that I cried in her lap.

I don't know if she meant it all or not. It could be that she just said all that to make me feel better, so that I do not fuss about things. But, little does she know, I am only worried about Raghav. He is a real pain in my ass lately.

He is not ready to understand. I spoke to everyone – Ruby, Tanvi, and Tiger – on conference call about him last night till 3 a.m.

"Naina, Veerain is here. Come out now," Neeraj bhaiya comes to tell me.

Shit! I am not ready. My hair is still wet. I have worn a white embroidered suit, and only put on kajal and eyeliner so far. I hurry with my slight makeup and wear my heavy antique coordinated earrings.

Mummy barges in. "Beta, he is waiting. You are looking pretty. Come with me."

"I haven't dried my hair!"

"It is your first personal meeting with him," she tells me. "It will be rude for you to make him wait. Come with me right now. You look perfect." Mummy drags me out of my room, not even allowing me to check myself one last time in the mirror.

Veerain stands up as soon as he sees me. I stand shyly in front of him.

Papa is not at home. Bhaiya and Mummy stare at us. I don't know how I am looking right now. Mummy doesn't know how cynical he is. He is very judgemental. He will judge my looks and snigger at me quietly.

I pretend to look for something on my phone while he talks with Mummy and Bhaiya. Seeing him there, sipping his juice, I think of sneaking back to my room to finish my touch-up. I take my chance.

When I come out, Mummy comes with a list of dos and don'ts for my meeting with Veerain. While pretending to listen to her heedfully, I look behind her... and catch Veerain ogling at me. He was checking me out.

We leave together in his Range Rover Velar – the same that I had banged into. I am loving sitting beside him in his car. Now I am getting that feeling of getting married soon. I am all smiles today. He is acting cool and chic, wearing his Emporio Armani goggles; I forgot to bring my shades

I feel very comfortable with him. The aura around him is so positive. There is no tension or pressure of any kind. I am myself when I am with him, and I do not hesitate to speak from my heart.

"Did he message you again?" Veerain asks me while driving. I am in a trance right now. My heart is full of happy songs.

"Who?" I ask him.

"Raghav, as you mentioned his name. You forgot his name quite quickly," he comments, bringing me back from my dream world.

"I don't keep wondering about him," I twit. This gets a chuckle out of him.

"By the way," I continue, "I blocked his number and all his unknown numbers after my last conversation with him." I do not want to go into details. I don't know yet if Veerain will trust me. What if he doubts my story, and feels like talking to Raghav first, before our marriage, to know both sides of the coin?

"All his unknown numbers? Why is he after you?" Veerain pries. This makes me sick. I really didn't want this conversation to happen.

"I met him a few days ago with my friends in a restaurant. He liked me there, and started clavering with one of my really good friends. He got my number from her later. And ever since then, he has been badgering me." I digest a lot of in-between information, which can prove to be fatal, if discussed this soon.

"You haven't met him once? Like, alone?" he asks casually.

I get tongue-tied. What shall I say now? Shall I be honest? What if he judges me? He looks at me with curious eyes when I don't speak. Shit! I am making him more suspicious.

"I have. My friends insisted on me meeting with him at least once. But I didn't feel anything for him. He behaved like a complete gentleman, though," I speak sheepishly.

"Oh! Like a gentleman! If he is so good, then what's the problem?" he asks.

And this makes me quiet. He is right. What is the problem? I hadn't really thought about it much, to be honest. It just didn't feel right to be with him.

"What happened?" he chimes in. "Okay. We are at the shop now. It is my family shop."

Uh oh. It's his family shop. Everyone here is going to judge me. Shit! I didn't know he was going to bring me here. His tauji could be inside.

Nevertheless, he walks ahead, and I follow him. Crossing through the door, we emerge into a big showroom.

All the staff members acknowledge him, and proceed to stare at me with utter curiosity. His Tauji is not here. Veerain escorts me upstairs to a special cabin, wherein we find a plump, stumpy man waiting. He seems to be the one in charge of this place. He orders coffee for us, and greets me very politely.

Veerain speaks to him, regarding and alluding to something. The man gives him a nod, and moves to the other side of the counter. He brings back a ring box.

Veerain has already selected the ring for me. It fills me with overwhelming emotions. The man leaves us alone now.

"This is a special ring," he says, looking at me and holding the box in his hand. "Our store has made only two pieces of this design."

He opens the box and takes out the ring to show me. And I get completely stunned. He smiles at me. And then his smile fades away.

"What happened? You don't like it?" he asks.

I don't know what to say. It is the same ring that Raghav proposed to me with. How do I tell him this? I hid this information from him. If I tell him now, he will doubt my credibility.

"I can't believe it that you don't like it. It is an exclusive piece of our store. The other one got sold in a day for fifteen lakhs. It has a ten-karat solitaire diamond," Veerain murmurs.

But all I can see now is that it is the same ring – the same ring that Raghav proposed to me with. This ring will always remind me of him, and not Veerain. It will never be mine and Veerain's ring.

"No. It is beautiful," I blurt out. "But it is too expensive. I am sorry. It is just too expensive."

"Why are you worrying about money? Just tell me, do you like it or not? It is from our store. I am going to put this ring only on your finger, on our engagement day. Let me take your finger's size now."

I can't stop thinking about Raghav and his proposal now. He said that he would come and talk to my parents. What will my parents think about me? Will they trust me when I say that I didn't encourage him?

"You look strained," Veerain murmurs, while putting the ring box back.

"I am just worried about Raghav," I tell him. "He is getting on my nerves."

"Why are you thinking about him right now?" he asks.

He is right. Why am I wasting my special moments with Veerain by worrying about Raghav?

"Relax. What can he do? Why are you worrying so much? Tell me, honestly," he asks caringly.

Aw! I want to say 'I love you' to him. But we haven't reached that stage yet. I don't yet know his feelings for me.

"He told me..." I begin hesitantly, "...that he would come to talk to my parents about..." I stall. It is not easy to tell your would-be husband that another guy wants to marry you, at any cost. I hope I don't scare Veerain away. His family has a reputation in the market.

"Naina, please, we are going to be husband and wife in a month. I am expected to know everything about my fiancée." He has a point.

"Raghav wants to marry me," I say. "He told me that he will come to talk to my parents about it. He thinks that no one can keep me happier and loved than he can. I don't know why. I didn't encourage him; trust me. I didn't give him any wrong impressions. He told me that he likes me, and I told him that my parents are looking for a groom for me. And that I'll be married soon. Then, all of a sudden, he came up with a marriage proposal, and he has made my life so difficult since then. I told him about you, honestly. Still, he is determined to convince my parents with his proposal." I open my heart to Veerain.

"What kind of a guy is he? He sounds crazy. Did you rebuff his proposal outright?" Veerain asks. Thank god, he doesn't think I am wrong. He is the best guy in the world.

"Yes, I have been very rude to him. But he doesn't seem to understand. I don't know what has gotten into his head, to behave so psychotically?"

"Do one thing. You want to eliminate all his drama, right? So that none of us, including your parents, get perturbed, and everything goes smoothly and happily? Talk to him," he suggests.

"What?" I grouch.

"Listen – hear me out first. Talk to him. Tell him that this relationship broke off due to some reason, and that your parents are now very upset because of it. The atmosphere in your home is really taut, and... and you are ready for his proposal. But you need some time for things to get normal first. And then, after some time has passed, you will talk to your parents about him, and introduce him to them." Veerain flashes a smug smile, but I am stunned to see his shrewdness.

"I told you that I do not play with others' feelings. I am not going to give him any false hopes," I tell Veerain straight away. His face wanes.

"Okay. Then let him humiliate you in front of your parents. They will think you are wrong. And please, let me know if this marriage is still on. In case your parents change their decision, let me know," Veerain murmurs, disgruntled.

I am not able to understand anything. Should I play with Raghav's feelings like this? How long will I be able to fool him with this ruse? He will surely come to know about my marriage eventually.

"Listen," Veerain explains. "I am also a guy. Judging his behaviour, I am sure that he is a crackpot, and is not going to sit quietly. Right now, only our families have agreed. Nothing is official until our ring ceremony. I want things to become official. Then, I will have every right to have a man-to-man talk with him. Trust me, if he decides to show your messages to your parents and spoil your image, you will have my backing. I'll vouch for you and tell them that I asked you to do this. It is just about five more days."

I agree with him. And both of us compose a message to send to Raghav.

Veerain and I go to Starbucks, and I chat with Raghav in front of him.

I didn't know Veerain could be this impish. He is enjoying this prank on Raghav so much. But deep down inside, I am feeling bad for Raghav. I don't know what the result of it will be.

But of course, Raghav also didn't leave me with many options. He was the one who threatened to involve my parents. He forcefully wants me to accept his proposal of marriage. Isn't that crazy?

Veerain and I spend some more time together. We mostly talk about Raghav, making fun of him and enjoying our prank on him.

Then, Veerain drops me at my place, where I go floating to my room. Mummy follows me, and inquires about my afternoon. I tell her about the ring, and she grows hugely surprised and impressed with Veerain. After lauding Veerain's character and qualities to Mummy, I send her out of my room, and lie still in my bed.

I am missing Veerain already. He gets a dimple on his right

cheek when he beams. It felt so heart-warming to laugh with him. I wanted to touch his hair. I am falling in love with this man. His lips are pinkish. He is so sexy. Will he be my husband? Really? Ah, it's like a dream. I love you, Veerain.

I want to text him something. I want to talk to him more. I open his chat on WhatsApp. His last seen is hidden, and he has saved my number now. I open his DP and kiss it.

I send him a simple message: *Hi, done with dinner?*

Oh god, it sounds so cheesy and passé. But now I can't undo it. I wait for him to come online and see my message. I stare at my screen for thirty minutes, before finally putting my phone aside.

I want to talk to him. I pick up my phone and check again – still no blue ticks. I am getting impatient now. I need to focus on something else.

I open my cupboard to pass time. I don't even know what I am looking for. But thank god, I start to calm down. I start selecting all the clothes I'll take with me to my new home. I had't realised I still have so much work to do. My marriage is in a month. And I have end term exams coming soon; I have to prepare for those, too.

And yeah, it doesn't even matter now if I score poorly, because I am not going to get a job based on my CGPA.

My phone chimes, interrupting my thoughts. I dash back over to grab my phone. Holding my breath, I open WhatsApp.

What are you doing? I want to hear your voice, Raghav texted.

Shit! I even opened his chat. I chatted with him like four hours ago. Is he mad or what? Don't I have anything else to do, other than chatting with him? I hope he doesn't call me now.

I check Veerain's chat. Still no blue ticks. Should I ask him to turn on his last seen on WhatsApp? Would that be too much to ask for, too soon? Yes, I guess so.

He comes online. Veerain comes online! And he stays online for nearly two minutes... but he doesn't open my chat.

What? He ignored my message. This means it could also be possible that he had come online earlier, but didn't read my message. Why is he ignoring me?

I call Ruby and tell her everything. We also add Tanvi onto the conference. Both of them take Veerain's side.

According to them, he would be busy at work right now, as he spent half the day with me. And he also has to take care of all the wedding arrangements. And they greatly love the idea of the prank on Raghav. They are so excited to meet Veerain now. They ask me to focus on the important work at hand. Tomorrow, I'm going to go shopping with them. For the next four days, I'll be busy shopping. Tanvi's mom will design all the dresses for me. For others, we will buy clothes from the market at a reasonable price. Then, I also have to go to a salon. Ruby will book my appointment.

I continue to talk to them for four hours. After that, I open Veerain's chat once again.

He replied an hour ago – *Yes, I did.*

I keep the phone aside. He just replied with this, and nothing else. Nothing about today's meeting. Nothing about marrying me. Nothing.

The next day, all the girls and I meet up at Tanvi's mom's store. Tiger is going to join us later for lunch. Tanvi got all the wedding dresses brought up here from her mom's factory – even the collection that is not yet displayed. I love her so much. Ruby, Tanvi and I all begin the arduous task of shortlisting the dresses for my ceremonies.

"Are you okay?" Ruby pries. "Don't tell me you are still fussing over Veerain?"

What shall I tell her? That Veerain doesn't seem interested in me?

"You are not okay. Did you talk to Veerain?" Ruby asks again, pulling my arm to force me to face her.

"No. He did reply to my message, but very tersely and formally. And since then, no message," I drone gloomily.

"Oh, that doesn't sound good," she mutters.

Tanvi comes with our coffee in white paper cups, and we settle down.

"What happened, dudes? Who is dead?" Tanvi gasps. She is taking a lot of pain to make things perfect for me.

Ruby and I exchange a look, and she notices us immediately.

"She thinks Veerain is not as enthusiastic as he should be," Ruby explains.

"Are you guys mad? When we are so busy, I don't even have time to breathe properly. Think of how busy he would be!" Tanvi squawks.

This doesn't convince me. And I really don't even want to explain this to anyone.

Neither Ruby nor I react to what Tanvi has said.

"Okay, give me your phone," Tanvi continues, proffering her hand.

"No." I know why she is asking. She still snatches my phone away, forcefully.

Just at that moment, my phone starts ringing.

"Whose is it?" I ask her with trepidation.

"I don't know. It's an unknown number," she replies.

"Don't pick it up. It will be Raghav," I bawl. "He has been messaging me since last night."

She waits for the phone to cease ringing.

"Please, Tanvi, don't! I beg of you. This is something serious," I shout at her.

"Yes. This is something serious. This is what I mean," she retorts, clicking on my phone.

She is calling Veerain, I know. Just the thought of it gives me the goosebumps.

But he doesn't pick up the phone, I guess.

But Tanvi calls again. "Tanvi, stop it," I bawl at her.

"Tanvi, let it be!" Ruby screams, too. "We don't know him yet. He could be busy!"

This makes me nervous. Tanvi shouldn't be interfering like this.

"This is what I said," Tanvi ripostes. "Hi, Veerain. You don't know me. I am Tanvi, your bride's bridesmaid," she chortles into the phone.

I have my heart in my mouth. I follow her to hear every word.

"Your bride is very unhappy with you. You are not giving her the attention she deserves. What kind of a husband will you be?" she says teasingly.

"That's no excuse. I am sending you the address of my store. We want you here in half an hour." She sounds demanding.

"No. You have to help us out. We are selecting her outfit for your ring ceremony. And also, we haven't met you. We want to meet you. You haven't gotten our go-ahead yet." She speaks like a child in a dulcet tone. "Really? That's so uncool. You are boring."

She says anything. I scowl at her.

"Really? That's okay. I can wait. Yeah, you are special," she natters with him rejoicingly. This baffles me. Is she really talking to Veerain?

"See. Problem solved," she beams at us, disconnecting the call. "He apologised for his absence throughout our shopping, but he will stay connected with us through our WhatsApp group. He asked to send him the shortlisted outfits – except for the bridal dress, obviously – and he will choose for you." Tanvi blurts all this out joyously.

My next three days are completely devoted to shopping. Tanvi and Ruby have been my constant companions. I am so relieved because of them. There is no way I could handle all of this on my own. Especially with so much stress. To add to it, Veerain has not been behaving properly with me.

He never calls or messages me on his own, but he does reply on our WhatsApp group with Tanvi, Ruby and Tiger. He even finalised my dress and sent the picture of his outfit for our ring ceremony on the WhatsApp group. But I am not feeling the connection with him like I should. He doesn't care for me.

My heart cries. I have an appointment in a salon right now. Ruby is coming to pick me up. Tanvi will meet me later in the evening.

But I can't share this feeling with anyone. I feel ashamed that my would-be husband is not interested in me. I don't want to go anywhere. I weep in the washroom for some time. I am really hurt because of him. Every morning, I get up in the hope of finding a sweet message from him, but in vain.

The whole day, I wait for his message or a call, but none ever come. And whenever I message him something, he replies so late and so formally. Why is he marrying me, if he feels so little for me? His blithe behaviour is killing me from the inside.

All these foretellings... the kundali is a whopper; Guruji is a fraud. There is nothing like a prophecy. Veerain doesn't like me. And I am going to marry him soon. Guruji told me that I'd marry my lover from the previous birth. It all sounds like trash now.

I come out of the washroom and find my phone ringing. It would be Ruby. But no... it is Raghav. I haven't picked up any of his calls or replied to any of his messages since that day. It's been four days. I still don't pick up his call. I have no strength to hear his nonsense and cheesy talk. I blame Veerain for all of this. I shouldn't have agreed to playing this prank on Raghav.

Raghav starts sending texts again on WhatsApp. What is wrong with this guy?

I open Raghav's text:

This is heights, Naina. How can you play with someone's feelings? You lied to me about your rishta being broken. I know you did all this to keep me at bay. But no. You can't play with my feelings and go like that. I am coming to your home tomorrow morning. I could never think that you... you could do this. What happened to the innocent girl I fell in love with? What happened to my Naina? Why are you doing this? To marry some guy you don't even know? What is wrong with me? Why don't you want to marry me? I love you so much. Why don't you believe it?

His words shake me to the core. I read the message twice, thrice. Isn't he right? Why am I marrying some guy who doesn't even care about me? And Raghav, he loves me so much. Why didn't I fall for Raghav?

"Hey, come, let's go! Sorry I'm late." Ruby comes to take me to the salon. I do not say anything to her. I need to know what I want. What am I doing with my life?

13

I need to talk to Veerain. I can't sort all this out on my own, when it concerns him too. When I am done with my facial, de-tan, and hair spa, I hand over my wallet to Ruby to pay the bill, and tell her that something very-very important has come up, and I have to make a call.

I call Veerain. Tonight, he will have to answer all my questions.

He picks up in one go. I thought I would have to call him a hundred times to make him answer my phone.

"Hello?" He answers in a curious tone. I immediately get tongue-tied. "Naina, is everything alright?" He sounds disquieted.

"No. Nothing is okay." A tear falls down my cheek.

"What happened? Is everyone fine at your home?"

"Why are you marrying me, Veerain?" I ask him finally. My voice is wobbly.

"Are you crying? Oh god, Naina, you are scaring me. What happened? Please tell me."

"I can't feel any connection between us," I say, firing my emotions. "Tomorrow is our engagement, and in a month, we will be married. But I don't feel a bond between us—"

He interrupts me mid-sentence. "Naina, please, stop it! Don't behave like a pampered child. Your parents, me... we all expect you to behave maturely. You know that I am busy. I told you when I met you that I stay busy. I am the only one in my family who has to take care of our business. I don't have a father to look after things so that I can relax a little and chill with my friends. I have given my sweat and blood to earn what I have today. I didn't have a normal, fun-loving life like you. What do you think? Don't I feel like taking a break, going out with my friends or being with a girl? Like all the other boys of my age? Life is not as simple as you think it is. I am sorry," he says exasperatedly. I hang up and cry. He spoke so rudely. All I was asking for was a little attention. Doesn't a girl have the right to know her would-be husband more closely? He calls back.

"Hello," I say whimperingly.

"Naina, I am sorry for venting out my frustration on you. Tomorrow is our engagement, and tonight I ruined your mood. I am sorry. I get your point, and I promise that, after tomorrow, I'll start taking out time for you. We both need to know each other in a better way." He coos lovingly. His sweet, caring voice mends my heart. He asks me about my preparations for tomorrow, and discusses his ideas for our wedding. It cheers me up.

Raghav's message suddenly pops up in my head. Should I discuss it with Veerain? Raghav is ireful. He will definitely show up at my house tomorrow and create a scene. If nothing is done now, then everybody's mood will be spoiled.

"Veerain," I say softly, "I got Raghav's message today, in the afternoon."

"What did it say?" He gets serious.

"It said he would come to talk to my parents tomorrow."

"This guy. Does he have a stop button?" Veerain gets stressed. After all, this was his idea. But all of this is happening because of me. I should have handled Raghav. Veerain has nothing to do with all of this.

"Do one thing. I am sending you a text. Just forward it to him. Okay?" Veerain says sternly.

"What text?" I am flabbergasted. What now?

"Just do as I say. And after that text, simply block him. Also, send me the screenshot of your chat once you have sent him the message. And do not worry. I am with you in this." He sounds very sure and unwavering.

After talking to him, I come and sit in Ruby's car with Tanvi. While waiting for Veerain's message, I narrate to them the entire scene.

We are getting late. The mehendi artists must be waiting at my home.

I get Veerain's text – *Dude, I am Naina's would-be husband. I want to meet you. Why don't you join us at our ring ceremony tomorrow, at the Sheraton Hotel, at 6 p.m.? Let's have a man-to-man talk, and you can tell me your problem, because clearly, you are not getting it the polite way. See you there!*

It sends chills down my spine. My body quivers. I am in no way sending this text to Raghav. Veerain has gone mad. He doesn't know who he is dealing with. I get Veerain's text, asking for a screenshot.

Tanvi takes Veerain's side. She says that this is the only way to handle a guy like Raghav. And when Veerain is with me, why am I scared? But I do not want to create a scene on my engagement day, in front of all our families and relatives.

Before I can think anymore, Tanvi snatches my phone and sends Veerain's text to Raghav, then blocks his number.

"Are you out of your mind?!" I squawk at her furiously.

I lash out at Tanvi in my agitation. Ruby intervenes, and takes us both to Tanvi's place.

After some time, I calm down and apologise to Tanvi, who is still sullen at me.

I lighten her mood by teasing her like I always do, and pack her stuff for a night-stay at my place. Ruby had already dropped her stuff off at my place, when she had come to pick me up.

We reach home. And Ruby starts getting calls from unknown numbers, because my phone is switched off. But we do not fret. Tonight, we will only chitchat about a happy tomorrow!

Next day, it is chaos in my house. Everyone is running to and fro, and grumbling about things left to be done.

I am almost ready. Veerain and I are going to be dressed in dark blue, coordinated outfits, and all my family members will be dressed in golden. It was Ruby's idea to have a dress code for family members. Veerain's family is going to be donned in baby pink.

I feel like a princess. Everyone is busy, except for me. Right now, three people are working on me – a make-up artist on my face, a hairstylist on my hair, and their assistant on my nails.

Tanvi and Ruby are ready, too. They are helping Mummy and Bhaiya to get the gifts loaded into the cars. We will leave in half an hour.

I am elated. Today is my engagement with Veerain, the guy I fell in love with in the blink of an eye.

My heart is throbbing. I was on pins and needles this morning, thinking about Raghav. I had a feeling that he would definitely show up at my doorstep. But he didn't. Veerain's idea worked.

We leave for the hotel, and I sit with Ruby and Tanvi in Ruby's car. Tiger is about to reach the hotel. I am so excited! I have butterflies in my stomach. My fingers are crossed.

I make my way to the bride's room, furtively, with cover from my besties and cousins. Veerain's family is already here at the hotel.

Tanvi is teasing Veerain over the phone. He is ignoring her now. She is ordering him to send his picture. I hope that, after today, everything changes for the better.

Veerain's ceremony has begun, and I wait with bated breath. Bhavya comes to meet me. Tiger is here, too. My cousins are approaching to congratulate me. Everyone is clicking pictures. But I am feeling a bit uneasy under the thick layer of makeup and heavy apparel.

Mummy comes to take me out. Oh, god! Now is the time. Everyone gathers outside the room to escort me to the stage.

'Din shagna da' plays in the background. My heart starts pounding fast. Mummy and Bhavya walk along on either side of me, holding my arms. Tanvi, Ruby, Bhaiya, Tiger and all my cousins follow behind us. I look at the people we pass with a fleeting glance. We stop in front of the stage, so that everyone can dance a little. I am feeling like a flower, surrounded on all sides by buzzing bees. I see Veerain standing alone on the stage, looking at me, holding his breath. Our eyes meet, and I fall deeply in love with him all over again. He is looking like a prince. He doesn't take his eyes off me. As if he's seen me for the first time.

We all move ahead, and then my procession leaves me alone to climb the stairs. I am quivering. I fear that I will fall. But Veerain comes forward and offers me his hand. Everyone hoots when I hold his hand.

Gently, Veerain brings me closer to him. I look at everyone in the hall. They all are cheering for us. I look back at Veerain. He is feeling shy, just like me.

Soon, all the ladies of his family come around us and ask Veerain to step down. My *godh-bharai rasam* starts.

I feel special and overwhelmed throughout the rasam. I am feeling so much love and desperation for Veerain now, in my heart, that there is no place for fear. After the ritual has concluded, Veerain steps onto the stage. Just he and I. He smiles at me shyly.

We exchange our rings amidst a shower of rose petals. Some people bring forth a three-storied red-velvet cake, decorated with white and red roses on all the steps, and a couple dressed in blue on the top.

My heart is absolutely overwhelmed, and tears begin to fall down my cheeks. I move to quickly wipe them away, but Veerain sees me. He holds me from my waist, and together we cut our cake.

After that, our photoshoot begins. I am feeling ticklish, and Veerain is all red. The photographer gives us such cheesy Bollywood poses. I can feel Veerain's breath over my forehead. For the first time, he holds me so tight and close to him.

In the middle of our schmaltzy laughs and talks, I catch a glimpse of Raghav. I stand stiff. Veerain is talking to Tanvi, Ruby and Bhavya near the stage.

Raghav is lunging through the guests, and emerges to stand right in front of me. He has bloodshot eyes, and I see the fire in them, which can burn down all of this. He looks at Veerain in indignation. Veerain notices him, too. I go and stand behind Veerain.

Somebody calls out Raghav's name. That's Veerain's Taiji. Veerain's Taiji and Tauji come to talk to Raghav. Do they know him?

I look at Veerain. Raghav doesn't take his incensed eyes off Veerain's face. I am quivering with fear. Veerain's taiji calls my parents, and introduces Raghav to them.

Raghav touches my parents' feet. What is happening? Veerain knows him? Raghav steps toward the stage, and begins to ascend. I can't feel anything in this moment. A little push can send me tumbling.

Raghav looks deeply hurt. I can see the pain in his eyes. He has subdued a storm within his chest.

Veerain comes to my side. I look towards him, to explain all this to me. He kisses my hand and shows my ring to Raghav. Raghav grits his teeth. I take my hand out of Veerain's clench.

"This is your *bhabhi*, big brother," Veerain says caustically to Raghav.

Brother? Veerain puts his arm over my shoulders. I shake him off, and he smiles sheepishly at me.

Raghav steps forward, but Veerain slides in-between us, asking a photographer to click our picture.

Tanvi and Ruby are equally shaken right now. Ruby goes to my mom to inquire about Raghav. Veerain and Raghav mutter something bitterly to each other, and then Raghav walks off.

He turns around once to look at me, before finally stepping down. His glance kills me. I feel like the most despicable person in the world.

I do not let Veerain touch me after that. He notices the defiance in my behaviour. I do not care about hiding my discomfort. I perform all the rituals and greet all of his family members with a feeble smile. All the elderly people are jovial. None of them knows how betrayed and deeply hurt I am feeling right now because of Veerain's blatant lie. I want to throw this ring in his face and walk off.

I still don't know Raghav's relation with Veerain. I am guessing that maybe he is his Tauji's son, just like I am Bhavya's cousin. How closely related they are, if this is true! How could Veerain do this to Raghav? If I had known about this relation, I would have never agreed to this marriage, despite my feelings for Veerain.

He used me like a pawn. He has been playing with our feelings from the beginning; both mine and Raghav's. How could you, Veerain? There cannot be any good reason for doing this. I don't want to marry you now. I am ashamed of myself for loving you.

When we come home, I do not speak to Ruby, Tanvi and Tiger. They get it. I just want to be alone. All our guests leave and I go straight to my room and lock myself inside. I want to cry, but not a single drop of tears falls. My head is exploding. I want to sleep, but I can't stop thinking about what Veerain has done.

He calls, and I do not pick it up. I want to talk to Raghav. But what possible excuse could serve to make him feel better? I have no words to apologise to him. He tried so hard to impress me, to win my heart... but I was blinded by Veerain's charm.

Veerain keeps calling me at small intervals. He drops me messages, too. I do not pick up his call or read any of his messages.

I stay in my room for two days, without talking to anyone unless it is supremely necessary.

I don't know what I want now. I can't marry Veerain. I don't think I can forgive him, either. I've gotten eight missed calls from him in the last two days.

Mummy knocks on my door. She tells me that Veerain and his mom are coming here, to talk about something serious.

I get up immediately to take a shower. Why is he coming with his mom? Are they coming to cancel the wedding? It will be very humiliating for my family. But what else could be the reason for a sudden visit?

My body starts to shiver due to the tension and mental pressure. I need to munch on something. I cut a mango for myself, and help Mummy to tidy the house.

14

Veerain and his mom arrive. I stand beside Mummy. Dad is not at home, and neither is Bhaiya. How are Mummy and I going to possibly handle this? Veerain looks at me. Our eyes meet, and it feels like I am seeing him after months.

He has got a beard. This is the first time I am seeing him with one. He looks damn hot. *Stop it, Naina. Just stop it.*

I go to the kitchen to make tea for Mummy and Veerain's mom, and coffee for Veerain and myself. I take the tray of cups outside and serve them all. "Naina, beta, get some snacks," Mummy implores me.

"No, no. I'm having the tea only because you insisted," cuts in Veerain's mom. "I don't drink tea at this hour – and snacks, please, no. Beta, come and sit with us."

I sit beside Mummy. What has happened to Veerain? He has been staring at me ever since he arrived. I feel extremely awkward. I look over at him, and he is still glaring at me. Is he trying to allude to something?

"Shall I consult about this with our pandit ji? Maybe he can come up with some remedy," Mummy suggests. What has happened?

"Behenji, I have confirmed this ten times from different pandits. And Veerain says it will also be easy for him to manage everything.

All the arrangements for the ring ceremony were done in haste. I don't want to be hassled about the other functions. I have only one son. I want to enjoy his wedding. Also, Veerain has to take care of everything all by himself. I saw how tiring it got for Veerain, having to book everything, shop for gifts, design invites and send them all out. But with a two-month period, everything will be managed perfectly, and we all will get a chance to enjoy ourselves." Veerain's mom speaks in a mellow fashion.

Oh! They have come to postpone the wedding. Two months now!

"Beta, you don't have any problem or objection with it? You are okay with it?" Veerain's mom asks me. I nod back at her.

"She has her exams in two days," Mummy replies. "Yeah, it will be very easy for everyone to prepare for the wedding now."

Veerain and I make eye contact inadvertently. And I look down immediately. I don't want to give him the impression that I have forgiven him.

"Aunty, I am planning to redecorate my room," Veerain says to Mummy very politely. "So, I wanted to take Naina's opinion for it. If you don't mind, can she come with us to our home? I'll drop her back here in the evening."

I am shaken. Why this, all of a sudden? Mummy seems perplexed too.

"That was our time when meeting our fiancé was impossible," puts in Veerain's mom. "But in today's time, kids don't follow that aeons-old culture. And I believe that we should also not foist our thinking and culture on them. I feel it is good if they get to know each other well, before their wedding. Also, I'll keep calling Naina to my home. I need a daughter to take care of my house. That's why I was so impatient to have the wedding in a month."

Hearing her pleas, Mummy isn't able to refuse and agrees with this.

After getting ready with very little make-up and donning a decent kurta, I leave with Veerain and his mom. Veerain's mom asks me to sit in the front next to Veerain. I shyly refuse, but she insists. She is such a cool mom. Veerain is so lucky to have her.

While driving, Veerain looks over at me many times, but I do not give any response. He plays all kinds of romantic songs on the stereo. Why is he acting so romantic today?

When we reach his home, Veerain's mom asks me to call her 'mom', just like Veerain does. It makes me feel comfortable and more attached to her. She is a gem. She shows me around their garden, drawing room, and kitchen. Their home is a duplex; Veerain's room is upstairs. After showing me around, she casually asks Veerain to take me upstairs.

I get butterflies in my stomach, but still... it doesn't make me excited to be alone with Veerain. I am deeply hurt by what he did. I am not the girl he wanted to marry; I am just the girl he didn't want Raghav to get and I don't know why. But he has used me to get back at Raghav.

"Come, this is our room." He's calling his room 'our' room now. It boggles me. I snigger, which he doesn't like.

"Naina, I brought you here because I wanted to explain. You didn't leave me much choice. You have been ignoring me like hell." He speaks exasperatedly.

So, my ignoring worked. I do not reply. I just walk past him, like he is not even there.

"I know I hurt you badly," he continues, blurting out in growing desperation. "You must be feeling betrayed. But you will thank me later, when you will learn what kind of a boy Raghav actually is. I literally saved you."

"Oh!" I spin back to face him. "So, you did all this to save me from Raghav? I didnt have to get engaged to you, to get saved from him. Right now, you are looking more of a devil to me than him."

My barb pierces into his heart. His face wans.

I go out to his balcony. I need fresh air to ponder. Should I marry this schemer? He is so manipulative and vindictive. A liar. He acts masterfully to look well-mannered, cultured and obedient to the world outside. No one knows about this side of him, except Raghav and me. And now he has the nerve to blame Raghav for all of this. I scoff.

"I lost my dad when I was six." I hear his voice as he follows me to the balcony and sits behind me on a pouffe. I do not turn around to face him.

"Since then, I have become very attached to Mom and Tauji. My Tauji literally took the place of my dad, for me. At that time, we all used to live under one roof. Raghav and I went to the same school. But we could never get along, even though I tried my best. We would fight hideously, come to fists and blows. We would compete with one another in everything. Everyone in our school knew that we didn't like each other, in spite of living together in the same house. Mom always taught me to respect Tauji and Taiji. She told me how much my dad was attached to Tauji. Even Tauji raised me dearly. He never differentiated between Raghav and me. In fact, he used to punish Raghav for his devilish and insensitive acts against me. Seeing that he was Tauji's son, I rarely reverted.

"And though Taiji doesn't show this blatantly, she believes in her heart that I am the reason Tauji dislikes Raghav. She holds me responsible for the differences between the father and son. It hurts me to see this in her eyes. She sometimes doesn't treat Mom and me well. But it doesn't matter to us now. Only Tauji matters to us. He is like my father. After completion of my school, I joined Hindu College in DU, and then IIM Udaipur. I would come to Mom whenever I had a long weekend. I had been always eager to work with Tauji, and he had enthusiastically taught me everything. I started to work with Tauji as soon as I left school. And he, in turn, proudly taught me everything. Under his guidance, I opened my own company and my own brand. I worked on it day and night while studying in college. I worked for nearly five years on some projects. Then, one day, Mister Raghav came back after wantoning around for years in the US in the name of higher education, and threw me out of my office. On the very first day of his arrival, he came to my office in my cabin, sat in my chair, flung my files onto the floor, and when I arrived, he asked the guards to oust me. He dissed me in front of my own staff.

"That day, I gave up on all decency and regard for brotherhood. I held his collar." Veerain doesn't cry, but I can feel the pain in his voice.

He raises his forefinger and speaks further, "My soul cried that day, Naina. I will never forgive Raghav for that affront in my life. I died from inside. I know the way I pulled myself together after that incident, just because of my mother. I can't share all of this with her. She cares for him, too. It is the last thing for her to see that both of us are fighting. For her sake, I keep my feelings suppressed deep down. But that doesn't mean I don't feel that way. I am going to work my ass off in my life, to make Raghav look very small in front of me. That's my dream in life, apart from keeping my mom happy." He snuffles. And I do not speak a word. I want him to let his frustration out today. I can see how suffocated he has been. Maybe, after today, he will feel a little lighter. This is the first time he is sharing his heart with me, or perhaps the first time he has ever shared his heart with someone.

"Tauji disparaged Raghav's act. He divided the entire property after that incident, and I came with Mom to this house. He very honestly and sincerely bifurcated the family property and business. It's been six months since then... and I am relieved that I do not have to see Raghav that often now. I have been working my ass off since then to expand my business. And I am sorry I used you, too..." He halts and sighs. "To get back at Raghav. I am extremely sorry. But this is also a truth: I could never get a girl more cultured and lovable than you. You are magnificent, Naina. I didn't realise, in my rage to teach Raghav a lesson, that I was also playing with your feelings by hoodwinking my real intentions. But this doesn't mean I don't respect you. I might have agreed to marry you because of Raghav, but I realised later what a special girl you are." He gets up and comes forward, holding my shoulders. I feel tingly. My heartbeat increases.

"I noticed your beauty and manners when I came to your home to take you out for selecting a ring. And yeah, I already knew that Raghav had taken the similar ring for someone, and that's why I actually asked the staff to make the same ring.

"But when I saw you on our ring ceremony day, walking towards the podium, my heart skipped a beat. I actually could not take my eyes off you. I got breathless. I could not believe my destiny that it had brought us together. I felt fortunate to be marrying you. And I honestly felt bad for playing with your feelings, and for hiding everything from you about Raghav. But it also gave me immense satisfaction to see his heart broken that day, Naina. That was the best day of my life." He speaks ecstatically. I leer at him for saying this.

"Naina, I really like you," he amends. "Please, forgive me and give me another chance. I want to restart my relationship with you. Please." He takes my hand, placing it over his heart.

"When you were walking through that aisle, I realised that soon you are going to be my wife – my life partner. I can't play with the emotions of my life partner. I have been desperate since then to tell you everything, honestly. And when you ignored me for two days – you made me go bonkers. I was so desperate to talk to you; and then I realised, thanks to Raghav, I had said yes. Otherwise, I would have lost the perfect girl for me. The way you tolerated my indecent behaviour, and the fact that I just easily shared my feelings with you, which I have never shared with anyone before, made me realise that you are the perfect one for me."

He kisses me on the lips, out of the blue. I have never kissed a guy before. My eyes jut out, as he closes his. I don't know what to do. I'm completely stunned. He doesn't let me go. I feel the twitch in my body. I close my eyes, and feel my heart pounding. I can feel his breath over my skin. His soft lips are pressing against mine. I sniff his perfume. His grip tightens on my waist. I get breathless – a current shoots through my entire body; as if my crotch is electrifying my body. I think my teats have reared. He kisses me for a minute, and then steps back and turns away his face. I turn away mine too, in abashment.

15

It was so difficult to look at Veerain after that. And he was intentionally staring at me. He knew he was making me shy. I thought he was a shy and quiet boy. But he certainly didn't seem like one today.

That energy flowing between us – that is what I actually wanted. It was so romantic in the car on our way back. Both of us would look at each other and smile bashfully. He wore a sweet smile after our kiss. I am sure his mom noticed that something had happened between us. And I think she was happy that it happened.

I love you, Veerain. I am falling head over heels in love with you. Please, do not break my trust ever again.

I get a message. It is from Veerain. I sit back in my bed.

I really liked bonding with you today. And it was my first time. I don't know about you. And it doesn't matter to me, how your past was. I just want to be your present and future.

Awwww. It was his first time, too. We both are so similar. I think of our kiss and feel a tingle in my belly again.

I text him back, and tell him that he is the first guy in my life.

We chat for some time, and I don't realise when it is 2 a.m. We stop when our eyes get watery, and we can't see the screen clearly anymore.

My heart is content now. But I am still eager to talk to him. It was our first real chat. He told me in detail about his school and college days. Girls he had a crush on, and how he used to react around them. His life's unique and embarrassing moments. About his friends, and all the fun times he had spent with them. And in return, I shared the same special memories of my own life with him. Now, I am feeling more attached to him. I doze off as soon as I close my eyes.

In the morning, I open Veerain's chat and wish him a good morning, adorably. My life has unexpectedly turned into a beautiful dream. I play romantic songs on my phone, and connect it to the speaker. I feel like caressing myself the way Veerain would love to do. Every part of my body is singing his name. I have replayed our kiss so many times in my head that it now seems more like imagination than reality. I wonder how will our second time be? Will he pull me towards him?

I spend my whole day chatting with Veerain rapturously. He replies late, but he does reply.

At night, while changing, I take a long glance at my body in the bathroom mirror, and try to see my bare skin through Veerain's eyes. How would I look to him? I touch my plump bosom and think of him. I want to become his.

I get a message from Veerain, he is too tired to talk or chat tonight. He is sleeping. I waited the whole day to talk to him.

To divert my mind, I look at the pictures from our ring ceremony day. We look so cute together. I kiss Veerain's picture on my screen.

I close my eyes and think of Veerain and me together. After some time, I see myself lying in a shallow pool. There is soft, mushy mud beneath my body. It is very dark, too dark to see anything clearly. But I can see *mashals* blazing on the mud walls. I realise that I am without clothes in this pool. There is no piece of cloth on my entire body - just the mud, cold and soothing over my skin. But I am wearing heavy bangles, almost up to my elbows. Why am I wearing bangles?

A rugged hand comes over my belly. The hand is rough and sinewy. He strokes my body gingerly, right from my chest to my crotch. It makes my groin twitch. His hand is skimming over my torso like a feather, and causing me to crave for him. I get pressed into the mushy mud as he weighs me down, with his body over mine. But I can't feel his weight. I am turned on. I can feel the fire igniting inside me.

Soon, I feel him inside me. It scares me first, then captivates me in the trance of pleasure. My body moans, and it makes him more thirsty for my flesh. My lower abdomen fills with frissons. I can't tell how many times my body got excited, but it doesn't end. It seems like the longest night of darkness swept over my skin, to knob my body till my last breath.

When he is finished, he separates his skin from mine. I see, with half-closed eyes, black water dribbling from his laboured body. I can't keep my eyes open for long. I close them, and open in a flash. I see his face – a face of horror.

I shoot up, gasping for air with my sweaty body. I have never felt more scared in my life before. Looking all around me, I still feel like I am sucked up in that mud. I get up and throw the quilt on the floor from my bed.

I sit on my bed dejectedly and think of that grimy dream. I feel like puking. My skin disgusts me.

I go to the bathroom and take a hot shower. The water is hot enough to burn my body.

It was Raghav's face. The same shrewd eyes, like those of an eagle. The way he looked at me... I want to kill myself. Why Raghav's face? Why? I slept thinking of Veerain. From where, then, did Raghav come into my dream?

I can't even dare to recall it in my mind. Every part of my body is feeling disgusted. I try very hard to fall asleep again, but I can't. I even change my bedsheet. But I just can't fall asleep. I am scared to see that dream again. No. It was yucky.

As a result, I didn't sleep the whole night. And now tomorrow is my first exam. I have six papers back-to-back. And I am exhausted. Thank god Veerain's mom postponed the wedding, otherwise I don't know how I would have managed it all.

I take Tanvi's help for all the concepts. Even Ruby is excellent in studies. I divide my entire syllabus in parts for Tanvi, Ruby and Tiger to explain to me. They happily agree to this. I also update them about everything getting normal between Veerain and me, and that he is on his best behaviour with me now.

Veerain tells me that he is there, in case I need help. While talking to Veerain over the phone, I think of the dream I had. Should I discuss it with him? No. It would be inappropriate, right? I just talk to Veerain casually. He tells me that he wants me to score well; otherwise, he will cancel the wedding, because he can't marry a dimwit.

I have always been good in my studies. But this time, it is different. I am not prepared. And my mind is f*cked up because of that filthy dream.

Somehow, I manage to appear for my exams with a calm mind. And I didn't see the dream again. Veerain talked to me every night, for half an hour. Tanvi, Ruby and Tiger saved me from flunking. They are the true saviours. Many times, when I was alone with either Ruby or Tanvi, I tried to talk to them about my filthy dream, but I couldn't spill the words out of my mouth. I think that was really for the best. Because the less I talk about it, the sooner I'll forget it.

Now, I can blab with my baby unlimitedly. My Veerain's world is so comforting, peaceful and easy-going. I am so, so very lucky to have him.

I want to meet with him but Papa and Mummy will not allow it, I know. But perhaps I could say that I am going to meet Tanvi and Ruby. Still, of course, they won't allow me to meet them right now, either. They have already made it clear that I need to focus on the wedding preparations right after my exams. Mummy will now resume her shopping with me, from tomorrow onwards. And with her there, I obviously can't ask Veerain to come and meet me. But I want our alone time. I want to kiss Veerain. I am dying to touch those lips.

At night, Veerain and I have a long conversation about random things. He asks me what I am planning to do after our marriage, and I tell him I am planning to be his wife.

He laughs, then asks, "Other than that?"

I don't have any answer to that. "What else?" I ask him.

"We all have a dream about what we want to be in our life. What is your dream? I want you to follow your dream; otherwise, you will just pester me to come home early and take you out for shopping, dinner or a party," he chuckles.

His sarcasm doesn't hurt me. He wants me to follow my dream. He is not asking me to leave everything behind and just focus on being his wife. He wants me to be something, to have my own identity. My first meeting with Raghav recurs in my mind. He had an interest in art, so he'd wanted me to have that same enthusiasm and zeal for art and to become his faithful follower and make him proud of me. I scoff at the thought. He thought I am pliable. I am glad that I am not with him today. I made the right choice, choosing Veerain over Raghav.

"Hey, where did you get lost?" asks Veerain, breaking my bubble of thoughts.

"Nothing. I just didn't think that you would ask me this," I reply.

"Why? What is so strange about this? I thought you would want to be independent and work your ass off to outshine your husband," he intones. He sounds exhausted.

"You got me right," I say. "Except for that outshining the husband part." In the middle of our prattle, I tell him about my family's objection to my working. He gets shocked to hear this. He says that obviously he would be worried about my workplace and environment there, to make sure of my safety, but nothing else aside from that.

I tell him that I'll join a company after our marriage, if he is okay with it... to which he agrees wholeheartedly.

After eventually hanging up the phone, I pray to god for everything to happen peacefully in my life. I want to marry Veerain. I don't know about my previous birth, or any lover. I just know that I love Veerain, and I want to become his.

The next day, I wake up a little early. I have to change my routine now, and inculcate a habit of following Veerain's routine. He leaves home at eight a.m. so, I will have to get up at seven to get his things ready and see him off.

When I go to the drawing room, I find Papa talking to someone over the phone. "Ji beta ji. We don't have any problem. You talk to Naina. It is wonderful. If your family is okay with it, then we don't have any issue... It is just that wedding preparations have to be done. Her entire shopping is pending. You can give some work to Neeraj, also. After all, he is Naina's brother. If we see, it was our duty, which you are taking care of. I am very much impressed with your sincerity, beta... Do give my good wishes to your mother, and to Tauji. God bless you." Papa hangs up, and looks at me.

My heart is in my mouth. Raghav hasn't done anything since my engagement. He hadn't even tried to contact me, after that.

"It was Veerain. Did you talk to him last night?" Papa asks me. What kind of question is that? I talk to him every night.

Mummy joins us, sitting on the sofa beside Papa. I perch on a chair. I need water. I am thirsty.

"Veerain just asked for my permission to allow Naina to join his office, as he needs a helping hand at work," he begins. "And he thinks, as Naina is free now, she can help him offload some work."

He breaks it as bad news, but every cell in my body gets charged up and begins bouncing with joy. I can't believe Veerain. He wants me to join his office! He even called Papa for permission.

I love you, Veerain. I can't believe my happiness matters to him so much. He will be the best husband. I couldn't ask for anything more. Seriously. I want to get ready and dart to his office right this instant.

Papa agrees to send me to his office. He says that Veerain was so persuasive, he couldn't deny the request – even though he wanted to. Papa asks me to tell Veerain that I should be home before 6 p.m. however, and that I will work only from Monday to Thursday – so that I can go wedding shopping on Fridays and weekends. When I interject and say that I can manage the shopping, he shows me his hand and asks me to do as he says.

Why do they have to interfere in everything? What will Veerain think of me? He takes his work very seriously.

Why didn't Veerain tell me about his idea of offering me a job in his office last night? But I loved the surprise.

I begin getting ready immediately, even preparing a light lunch for myself, and sprint for a cab. I've assured Papa and Mummy that it will be fine. I'll be home on time, and they've got to trust their would-be-son-in-law, if not me.

I reach Veerain's office. It is really beautiful and well-organised. I have never been to an office before. But this building is freshly constructed, and everything looks new and well-designed, just like the ones shown in movies. Everyone knows me here. They all greet me very cordially, and it fills me with confidence. I look at Veerain; he is all suited-up. My Veerain, with silky hair and a dimple on his right cheek.

He spots me, and a smile comes across his lips. He gestures to me to go to his cabin and wait. He is the boss here, and I am his fiancée. Veerain is so handsome; all the girls here would be jealous of me. And they might even have a crush on him. My heart starts thumping. How will I compete with them? What if they make me look inane to Veerain, and not worthy of him?

Can Veerain find me not good enough for him? Why not? He can. What if he cancels the wedding? I'll die. If Veerain left me, I'd die. Not because of shame, or what this stupid society and my parents would think – but because of the pain.

I can't see Veerain finding me unworthy of him. I cannot live without him now. Shit! Why didn't I think of all this before? I should never have come here.

Veerain enters. He is so happy to see me here. I tell him honestly that I don't know what to do, and how to do any work here. He tells me I will learn everything gradually, and that I only need to be attentive and agile. He has asked a staff member to train me.

For my first week in the office, I will be a trainee. And Veerain is always here to help me out. I can come and ask him about anything, anytime.

I nod to everything he says. I have to prove my worth to him.

I am led to my cabin. He has gotten a cabin ready, especially for me. This makes me feel so special.

I promise to work my ass off day and night, and show Veerain that I am the best girl for him. I can't let him down, and let him think that he has gotten stuck with a dork.

I do not think about what Papa preached in the morning. He can say whatever he wants. My life has begun now, and I'm going to have to fight my battles. I can't explain all of this to him, and it is difficult to ask edgy parents not to worry unnecessarily – because this is what they do. They worry needlessly and fetter you; they never let you do anything for yourself.

I don't even realise when it's time to go home. I don't want to go home; there is so much work left here. Mummy calls me, but I don't pick up her call. I am stressed out and irritated. I can't answer her stupid questions right now. I'll call her back at seven. and tell her that I'll be there by eight. Even if I have to fight my parents to let me work here, I will. Because this is what I want in my life. I want Veerain, and I want to make him feel proud of me. This is my life's goal now.

Veerain comes to my cabin and asks me why I am not picking up my parents' calls.

I roll my eyes and tell him I didn't notice. I call Mummy back in front of him. At first, she scolds me for not answering her calls, then tells me how worried she got. I want to snap at her, but I can't, not in front of Veerain. What is there to feel so concerned about? I am in the office, obviously, working. Yeah, but they don't trust their kid, and they would be probably thinking I am off sleeping with Veerain in some hotel room. Ughhhh!

I speak coldly to her. I am at work, for god's sake. Why doesn't she get it? Veerain asks me to cool down. He takes my phone, and tells her I am coming home, and that he will drop me himself.

This makes me feel pathetic. I know how busy Veerain is, and now, he will have to take me back home. He is definitely going to regret his decision of calling me here to work. I hate you, Mummy, for ruining my life.

Veerain notices my spoiled mood. He tries to cheer me up when we get into his car. He tells me stories about his mom, and how manically she acts sometimes. He understands that parents get over-protective sometimes. His own mom was no less, in the beginning. She would pester him to come home early, and she would not eat anything until he reached home. Slowly, she gave up on him.

He politely explains to me that I have very little time left at home to be with my parents, so I should be more patient and accommodating with them. I will miss them and their protectiveness after marriage. He doesn't have any issue with me leaving the office at six. He will even ask his driver to drop me home every evening.

Aw! I love you, Veerain. He makes everything so perfect and easy for me. I see the blessings of Lord Shiva in him. Thank god I kept the fasts. Maybe because of my fasts, I got such a good partner in my life. I can fast for Lord Shiva my entire life now, to keep Veerain with me forever.

I say 'I love you' to him, out of the blue. He gets thrilled to hear it. We reach my place, and I give him a quick peck on his left cheek and get out. He smiles like a kiddo. I blush, too.

I give him a flying kiss, stepping inside the porch. He smiles and drives away.

I do not bristle at Mummy for her behaviour, but very politely try and explain to her the environment at my office.

Mummy gets it really quickly, and she even suggests for me to buy some new and stylish formal outfits, and to be very attentive to Veerain.

It actually feels good to discuss my heart with Mummy. I hadn't thought that she would be able to get me this easily. She even gives me some fantastic tips to keep Veerain hooked up to me, like cooking something extraordinary and delicious for Veerain every day. She tells me it all will take some extra effort, but it will all be worth it in the end.

So, I get up a little early the next morning, cook something light and delicious for Veerain, and dress up all bonnily. I know how to turn all eyes to me. I can't look like a swot in his office. I have to be perfect in everything. After all, he is worth all this effort.

Veerain and I have lunch together. The whole day goes incredibly well. I bring one or two files home with me to work on them.

I actually come home early, so I have time to work on my outfit for the next day, a special dish for Veerain, and finish my office work sincerely at home, late into the night.

I am buried under an avalanche of work these days. I search for a good recipe every evening, and then try to cook it. Sometimes I have to toil for hours to perfect it. Then I spruce myself up, every morning, with attention to my nails, heels, hair, make-up and dress. I have to be pitch-perfect. Then the pile of office work. I get knackered by the time night descends.

I have worked so hard this entire week that my mind has stopped relishing anything. It just keeps running and fussing over the next thing I have to do, while I am on one thing. But Veerain complimented me today. He said that he is happy about his decision of calling me to work in his office. He is proud of me. And that's all that matters.

I can't suppress my yawns now. I am sleepy. My body is aching from all the rush to get things done perfectly. Veerain is happy with me, feeling blissful and content I doze off.

I see myself panting for him. I liked his touch. He is gone out of the pool, but my body is too feeble to pull myself out of the mud. But it is soothing on my sore skin. He shagged me, and I let him.

I glance around at the place from the pool. It is dark, ominously dark. I feel like closing my eyes and leaving my body free. Letting it float. But it is a shallow pond. I keep my hands beneath my hips, and give a deep sigh of relief. It's a long, tiring night, and I have no clue when it will be over. He comes again, and sits next to me. He lifts my body with his sturdy arms, and water, heavy with mud, dribbles down my skin. He takes me out of the pond and lays me down on a fabric. I don't know what is beneath me, but its touch is so soft. What is he up to? Why doesn't he get inside me?

My body has craved for a man for so long. And he gave me that love that I deserve. But I can't stay here for too long. I can't sleep with him every night. I get up and take a close look at his face. His eyes are brown. They have black magic in them. He comes closer. I feel his breath over my lips. He rubs his hand over my groin. I give a sigh of deep pleasure. He knows where to touch me. He has been playing with my body. When he reaches me like this, I crave for his touch even more.

He will never let me wake up. He, too, does not want this night to end. He is thirsty for me.

I wake up gasping. What is wrong with me? What is happening to me? I switch on the light. Everything is normal. But I am not normal. There is something wrong with me. I feel ashamed. I undressed in front of Raghav. I let him touch me. I can't even tell anyone about this. How can I? I am engaged to Veerain.

I empty an entire bottle of water onto my head. I sit on the damp floor in my drenched clothes and cry. What is happening to me?

Why am I seeing such dreams? Why Raghav? Had it been Veerain, it would still have been fine. But why Raghav? I give a loud sob and thrust my mouth into my knee to suppress my cry.

I never thought of Raghav in that way. I never imagined any such thing about him. I never saw him like that. Then, why?

16

I catch a cold. It was a horrible night. I cried the whole night. My head is exploding now. I didn't even change my clothes.

Mummy asked me to stay in bed, fetching me some ginger tea and giving me medicines to help bring down my temperature. She thinks all of this is happening because of fatigue and tension. But only I know why, and only I know how disgusted I am feeling with myself.

I am feeling pukish; my nose is running, and my throat is killing me. I take a pill to make my mind rest and lie down to sleep. I sleep the entire day. And I sleep through the night.

I didn't talk to Veerain. I am feeling so guilty that I can't talk to him about my dream. Guilty like I've cheated on him, and now I'm sheepishly trying to hide it from him.

I am in no mood for shopping. I tell Mummy that I'll go with her next week. She reminds me that there is only a month left until my wedding. We are yet to buy gifts for Veerain and his family. I have to buy new clothes to wear after my marriage. We have to shop for everyone. My 'daily-routine-stuff' list also has to be prepared and bought. There is so much work to do.

Papa got really angry yesterday that I fell sick and didn't go out shopping, but Mummy calmed him down. He said that was why he'd asked me to only go to the office four days a week, so that I could shop and rest during the other three days.

None of them know what is actually killing me from within.

On Monday, I tell Papa that I have some files with me at home. So, I'll go to the office today and return these files, and then I will join Veerain's office only after our wedding. Mummy asks me to take the car instead of calling a cab.

Ruby has been asking me about our mehendi performance. We are planning to have a joint ceremony for the ladies sangeet with Veerain's family. Thinking about this reminds me that Raghav will be there, too. It stops my heart. I try to divert my mind. I have to throw a cocktail party and bachelorette party. Do I even have the funds for so many parties?

A car gets in my way. The driver doesn't move it aside. It halts in the middle of the road. I have to take a left from here. I look closely; it is a Mercedes Benz AMG GT. Shit! It is Raghav!

It is definitely Raghav. I try and move my car, but as I try to reverse, his car comes closer, and stops head-on adjacent to mine. I should call Veerain.

I get Raghav's call first. He is right in there and calling me. I do not pick up his call. I look around for help. Raghav honks sonorously. I bang on my steering wheel. What does he want?

He gets out of his car, primped in all black, with svelte black shades. He comes and gets into my car. He sits next to me. I look at him in awe, and he pretends like nothing is unusual or inappropriate about this.

My car fills with his strong perfume. He doesn't say anything. I do not look at him again. He snuffles.

My heart is thumping.

"Take a left," he says, very calmly. I look at him in astonishment. I do as he says. His car is still parked in the middle of the road.

"Put it in neutral." He speaks tersely. He is in no mood for cracking jokes. He is serious. And I have no clue as to what to do.

"Look at me, Naina," he says to me. I do not look at him; I can't. Please, Veerain, call me. Mummy, call me.

He doffs his shades. And I look at him, and I see the same face I have seen in my dreams – the same jawline, the same thin pink lips and shrewd, almond-shaped eyes. He is clean-shaven today.

"Seeing me after a long time? Lock my angelic face in your heart. It's a rare beauty," he says with a smirk. I quickly jerk my head to look outside my window.

I saw his face carefully today, but never before. So, how had I seen this face clearly in my dreams, then? It is the same, exact face, from edge to edge. I feel a shooting pain in my skull. I hold my head with my right hand.

He chuckles. I roll my eyes.

"If you like me so much, then why are you marrying him?" he asks in his American accent. Ruby was charmed by this accent, but when I'd heard his voice for the first time, I felt like I had heard it somewhere before.

"Tell me, Naina. You are not going anywhere today, before you answer all my questions," he says sternly, but calmly.

I look at him. What? Is he going to keep me confined in my own car?

"I told you I love you. I told you how I feel about you. I told you that no one can ever keep you as happy as I can. And I very politely asked you to marry me. That son of a bitch was not even in the picture, when I proposed to you."

"Stop it. You can't abuse his mom like that. You should be ashamed of your language. She is your aunt!" I scream without looking at him.

"I am sorry. Yes, I shouldn't. Okay. Let's start it again." He is talking like a crackpot.

He turns to my side. "We met first, right, Naina? I liked you first. I approached you first. I gave you a ring first. That asshole even copied my ring." He laughs bitterly. He is full of spite for Veerain. He loathes him. "Why did you play with my feelings, Naina?" His voice suddenly gets hoarse. I know he is hurt because of Veerain and me. And why wouldn't he be?

"I am sorry," I say. "It is all my fault. I do not feel the same way for you, Raghav. I tried to explain this to you. But you were not ready to understand. You made everything so creepy for me. I wanted to tell you about Veerain, but you threatened me that you would involve my parents. I didn't want a scene."

He doesn't interrupt me. He is listening so attentively that it makes me nervous.

He licks his lips. "I still don't get why you are marrying him. Let me ask you very, very clearly. W-H-Y A-R-E Y-O-U M-A-R-R-Y-I-N-G H-I-M?" he drawls. He is really scaring me now.

I don't answer.

He bangs on my dashboard with his right hand, shocking me.

"Why are you marrying him, Naina?" he repeats, growing louder. "You don't want to marry me because you think you don't love me. Then, why are you marrying him? Why did you agree to marry him?" He is reciting the same question, like a kid recites a nursery rhyme.

"I don't know why I am marrying him. I just know I don't want to marry you. You are a psycho. Get out of my car, Veer... Raghav. I am out of patience for you now." Veerain's name was about to slip out of my mouth, instead of Raghav's. What is wrong with me?

I don't think he is going to listen to me. I don't want to call Veerain. Raghav is full of spite and anger for Veerain. I don't want a brutal fight. I can't call anybody else. Nobody knows about Raghav and me.

He chuckles.

"You are testing my patience, Naina. You don't know me. I'll kill Veerain. What he has done to me now... he crossed all limits by it. I can't forgive him. You were the last straw. He shouldn't have involved you," he mutters balefully. I am horrified. How could he say that?

I open the door and take a step outside. But he pulls me back in and closes my door. I stare at him in stark dismay.

He chuckles again.

"You can't marry him, please, stop it. You can stop it. Cancel this wedding, Naina. I swear to you that I will kill him. I can do that. But if you agree to cancel this wedding, nothing will happen. I love you, Naina. I will not let him snatch you away from me. I am a complete psycho. And I am fixated on you."

I open the door again. But once again, he forcefully closes it. I try to call somebody on my phone, but he snatches my phone away.

"I love you, Naina. You don't understand. My soul is attached to your soul. I can't forget you. It is not in my hands. Don't get restless. I know you don't believe me." He holds both of my hands. "You've got to spend some time with me. You will see what I have seen. We are attached to each other, Naina. You love me, but you just don't know that yet. You love me. You are supposed to be with me. Look at my face. Have you not seen this face in your dreams? Have you not heard my voice in your dreams? Don't make this mistake, Naina."

"Stop it, Raghav. Stop it! Just stop it! I can't hear your crap anymore; I can't. I don't have the bile to digest it. Please, leave me alone. I beg you, get out of my life. You repulse me. Yes, you do. I don't care about Veerain or anybody else. If it weren't Veerain, then it would have been somebody else. But not you. I just hate you. You disgust me. Get out of my car, right now!" I speak thunderously. I have had enough.

He swallows his tears. I see his bloodshot eyes. They scare me.

"Okay, then." He puts my phone on the dashboard and gets out of my car.

My entire body is trembling with fear.

Getting back into his own car, he puts it in reverse, and I breathe a deep sigh of relief when he is gone.

Moving and struggling with my quivering fingers, I call Veerain. He picks up. "Raghav came by to meet me," I cry out. "He confined me in my car. He got in forcefully. He has gone mad, Veerain. He has gone completely mad!" I burst out.

"Relax, Naina. Relax, calm down. Take a breath. First, breathe. Go to my house. I am coming home. Where are you right now?"

"I am halfway to the office. I am driving," I stutter.

"Go to my place. Stay there and relax. I am coming home. Okay?"

I drink some water and drive cautiously to Veerain's house. I am shaken to the core. How could Raghav say that? That he will kill Veerain. I can't believe him. Can he go that far? To kill his own brother?

I reach Veerain's house. But his car is not here. He hasn't arrived yet. I go inside. His mom is not at home, either. The help tells me that she will come by in the evening. She has gone to the temple, to attend a pooja.

I feel extremely peckish. I left my lunch in the car, and I don't want to go outside now.

I ask the help to give me a cup of coffee and an apple, and I go to Veerain's room. I lie spread-eagle on his upholstered recliner.

I try and watch TV to distract myself and sip coffee, but I can't stop thinking about Raghav's threat. When will Veerain come? I am getting suffocated now. My head is exploding with pain. I call him... and I hear his ringtone nearby.

I sprint outside, and bang right into him in the doorway.

"Hey, beautiful." A smile comes across his lips. He embraces me tightly. Oh! I was dying for this. At last, I begin to relax. My heartbeats calm down. He squeezes me, and then wraps his arms around my waist. We both look into each other's eyes. He brings me into the room, and kisses my lips amorously. I smile in-between our kisses. He rubs his nose over mine and pins me to the wall.

"Veerain, your help will come," I mutter. He stretches his arm and gives a hard push to the door. It shuts deafeningly.

He holds me tightly, and starts kissing me again. I feel the tickle in my belly. He pulls me in, from my waist. I can feel his urge to have me now. He is as thirsty for me as I am for him. I am melting in his arms.

He chews my lips, plays with my tongue and makes me gasp for air. He pats on my right hip and pins me back to the wall. We both stare into each other's eyes. I see my lipstick smeared all around his lips.

I can sense the vibes flowing between our bodies. He doesn't touch me anywhere else. But I can feel that his thirst hasn't quelled. He wants more of me. He brushes my lips with his thumb. I look into his eyes playfully. His eyes sparkle and his face gleams. He holds my hand and takes me to the bed.

We lie on his bed together. I feel his warm hands over my skin. My heart is throbbing. Our legs entwine. He grabs me in his arms. I feel very secure with him. I feel a relief, and a different kind of calmness in my body. He bares my bosom. And I see a look of awe in his face. It makes my mouth watery. He strokes me, bites me lovingly. I adore his every touch.

We both stop, pantingly, and look at each other's face. We kiss one last time, and get up. We only made out and it was breathtakingly awesome.

Today, I am not feeling shy to face Veerain. Instead, I want to keep looking at him. I want him to blush back at me.

He takes a T-shirt out from his wardrobe, and goes to the washroom. Would he be treating himself in the washroom? I think he enjoyed our short trip to heaven.

He emerges, all freshened up and wearing a thin V-neck T-shirt. He is looking hot, and making me hot. Now, I can't wait for our first time. Just twenty-eight days more, Naina.

"How are you feeling?" he asks me.

What kind of question is that? I redden. He flushes too. He runs his hand through his hair, and goes out of the room. Now it hits me: why I came here in the first place. A chill runs down my spine.

Veerain comes back gleefully, but his expression changes when he sees my face. I think he's read my mind.

"I am sorry, I completely forgot about it. Tell me, baby, what did that jerk say to you?" he asks me.

Did he just call me 'baby'? Gosh! It sounded so cute.

He steps forward to hold my arms, and sits with me on his bed.

"He came angrily, blocked my way with his car and got in forcefully." I start telling him what had happened. "He didn't let me step out of the car, and was blurting rubbish. He scared me, Veerain."

"Do you want me to have a word with him? I can do that. And you don't have to be scared of him. It is my mistake. I took him casually. I thought that he would run back into his shell, after knowing about our relationship. But no. He is a mutt. I'll have to tell him, in his way, to bugger off," Veerain intones.

This scares me even more. Our marriage is just a few days away. I don't want any drama around it.

"You go home; I'll call Raghav and talk to him," Veerain says to me.

"No," I say. "Maybe this is his plan. He knew I would tell you everything, and that you will call him to talk. He wants to create a scene, to hinder our wedding."

"He can't really do that, if that's his plan. And I can't trust him with you now, Naina. He is a mutt, and there is no limit to how low he can stoop. You need to be careful until the wedding." Veerain is concerned for me.

"You are worried about me. And I am scared for you. He is not going to do anything to me. He will try to hurt you," I accentuate.

"Why will he not do anything to you?" Veerain scoffs.

"I am scared for you. He said to me that he would kill you if I didn't cancel this wedding."

Veerain jeers. "He will kill me! That bastard has given me such threats many times before. Even right after our ring ceremony, I got his spiteful messages: to teach me a good lesson, kill me, beat me to death. We both got into a tiff over the messages, and then what? We blocked each other. Did he do anything after that? It has been three weeks since then." Veerain tries to explain to me.

"This is how you two talk to each other?" I am startled.

"What do you expect? We never shared a brotherly bond. We hate each other. Don't expect me to treat him like a brother," Veerain says gruffly.

I don't want any fight here. Least of all because of me. What will Veerain's family think of two brothers fighting over a girl? They will never want such a girl to come into their family. I don't want that. And Veerain will never get this.

"Especially when I have to go abroad. On Wednesday, I am going to Abu Dhabi for a business deal. I can't trust that rascal in my absence," he mutters.

He is going to Abu Dhabi day after tomorrow!

"And you are telling me this now?" I growl, scowling at him.

"I got to know on Sunday myself. That's why I wanted some special alone-time." He caresses my chin, but I turn my face away.

"For how long?" I ask. I can't live without him. I can't even think of him being so far away from me.

"Just for two days, baby. It will be fine," he says coyly. "And I will have to go on business trips after our marriage, too. I am going with a male colleague. So, there is nothing to freak out about."

It is not about that. I trust him blindly. I know he is completely into me, at least for now.

"I am worried about what Raghav is planning to do," I squawk.

"He is planning nothing. But I still want you to be safe. Stay inside the house. Why don't you come to stay over here for two days, while I am out? I think your parents will agree; it will require a great amount of efforts, but they will. And then, I will not have to fret about the well-being of the two most important ladies in my life," he says lovingly and kisses me again.

17

I gave him his files and met with aunty. She said she would call Papa tomorrow in the evening, to convince him to let me stay at their place for two days. Then, I drove back home. I don't know if Papa will agree or not.

It will be fairly easy for me to stay calm if I remain at Veerain's while he is away from me. I will feel closer to him there. I'll see his pictures, go through his things, and sleep in his bed. His bedsheet and quilt will have his smell, and that will work as a relaxant for me.

I will take care of Aunty, and talk to her about Veerain's life before I came into the picture. I really hope that Papa agrees. Please, it is high time. He shouldn't foist his opinion and outmoded thinking on us now.

I think of our special moments from today. Aww! I feel the same tickle again. It was so romantic. He literally chewed my lips. And I was melting like ice cream in his arms. I have never felt that way before. His kisses were different too; they were more passionate. He loves me. He really does. I dose off, dreaming about me and Veerain in our peaceful world.

The next day is a nerve-racking day for me. I keep agitating Veerain by calling him. What to do? I want to stay at Veerain's. I don't know if his mom will be able to convince Papa or not. He is very rigid and illogical. He can fiercely stick to his point without any sense or regard for others' happiness.

Every time Mummy's phone rings, I straighten up.

I am being really polite and attentive to Mummy, to impress her – so that when Papa refuses Aunty, Mummy can hopefully intercede to convince him. I even cooked today. She is really pleased with me. Somewhere, I am feeling guilty for tricking her like this. But the thought and wish to sleep at Veerain's is so tempting that everything seems fair right now.

I come to my room to call and talk to Tanvi. It has been too long since I last chit-chatted with my buddies. They might be wondering that I've changed since I met Veerain.

Tanvi's phone is ringing. And in the middle of it, I hear the ringtone of Mummy's phone. I get on my feet.

"Heyyyyyyyy, my munchkin! How is my baby?" Tanvi speaks jubilantly. Hearing her chirpy voice makes me nostalgic.

"I am sorry, darling. I called you to blab, but I have to go now. I'll explain it to you later," I say hurriedly as I go to stand outside Mummy's room to hear whom she is talking to.

"What? This is not fair," Tanvi grouses. "I wanted to talk to you. But then you were busy with your office. I want to tell you what is f*cking happening in my life."

"I know, baby. I miss you, too," I coo. "I'll talk to you tonight. I promise. Right now, I am in the middle of something, and I have to get it done. Please."

She says okay, but apathetically. It is okay; I'll cheer her up later.

I finally get ready to eavesdrop on Mummy's conversation over the phone, but she hangs up before I can make out anything. Who was it? Shit!

I get Veerain's call. Finally! I have been dying to talk to him.

"Hey baby! It was really hard to convince your dad," I hear him say. He sounds exhausted.

"Did he agree?" I squeak with joy as I shut my door.

"No, no. I don't know. Mom tried to explain it to him. If he is worried about me, that you and I will be under one roof for a night, then you can come to my place when I am gone. My flight is early in the morning on Thursday, so I'll leave home around 4 a.m. on Thursday. That's why I wanted to pick you up on Wednesday evening. But god knows what is on his mind? He said, it doesn't happen in our family; we don't follow such a culture. Honestly, Naina, when Mom told me about his statements and his tone, it really irked me. But then, thinking of you, I let it go. Now I am not going to ask him again. I can't ask Mom to call him again for this. I am sorry, baby. I thought that we could have some fun together. It is an era of live-in relationships. And we are goddamn engaged to each other. I am calling you with his permission to stay at my place in my absence with my mom. You tell me, what is f*cking wrong in this?" He is vexed right now.

"Yeah, I understand," I say sheepishly.

"Yeah, look, I'll talk to you later. I am drained. Talk to you tomorrow. Please, bye," he says rudely and suddenly.

After hanging up, I wonder if he was really rude, or just tired and agitated with my dad. But thank you Papa, for ruining everything.

I don't go out to Mummy's room. I know what she will say. She will only second and echo papa. All the frustration that I have inhibited in my heart due to them starts coming out.

I feel scared sometimes, that I might burst out in front of them someday. What would that be like? They won't be able to take it, I am sure.

I spread all my clothes on the bed in frustration. After some time, Mummy comes in to talk to me. I do not look at her face. She gets it; I am in a snit. She tries to talk about random stuff, but I do not respond. She leaves my room in despair.

They wanted me to get married. Did I say anything? They did not want me to get a job. Didn't I give up on that? Then, luckily, they and I fell for the same boy. Seriously, this is my luck. Otherwise, they would have selected a guy of their choice, irrespective of my preference, and forced me to marry him. And now, when everything is perfect, why do they have to create unnecessary problems? If they stay like this, will Veerain like them in the future? I am boiling with agitation right now.

I don't go out of my room, even when I hear Papa's voice. I am cursing my life. Even when god wants to give you happiness in your life, your parents come in between.

Out of the blue, I start wondering about Raghav's threat. I'd completely forgotten about it. Also, I didn't get a dream about Raghav after Friday. I think there is some serious problem with me.

I flake out, listening to my favourite songs.

In the morning, the first thing I see is Veerain's message –

I am sorry, baby. I shouldn't have reacted that way. I can understand why uncle said all that. It is all cool. And I need to do something with my anger problem. See you soon, angel. 26 days to go, and then you will be mine forever!

I get ecstatic. He is my man. I send him many kisses with an 'I love you' voice note, and all my anger for Mummy-Papa winds down. Rather, I feel guilty for having had all those bitter thoughts for them last night.

I go out of my room. Everyone is sitting there and they look at me in unison. What? Were they talking about me? Papa quietly observes me first, then asks me to sit with him. He tells me about Veerain's mom's call that he'd received, and also about his reaction to it. Mummy also joins in. Bhaiya is running late, so he leaves for his office.

My parents both give me disguised advice about not losing my virginity. I don't know how to react to it. Why are Indian parents so obsessed with their child's virginity? What do they have to do with their child's sexual life? It is crazy and creepy.

But the ultimate conclusion of this entire conversation is that they are ready to send me to Veerain's house this evening. Whoopee!

After Papa is gone, I come to my room to call Veerain. I tell him to pick me up after his office. He is just as surprised by this new turn of events as I am.

I start packing my stuff for a two-day stay at Veerain's. I can't believe it! Ever since Veerain has come into my life, it has changed completely. I hadn't thought that I would get this eager and exuberant for my marriage. I was always so negative about it.

Now, focusing on clothes, who am I going to spend my night with? With his mom, or with him? For the daytime, I pack Indian attires. But what about tonight? Veerain had blurted out in his anger that he was planning to spend this night with me.

Anyway, I pick out a special dress for tonight, in case I am with him. If I'm not, then this dress can wait for another month. Ah! I am so excited.

At 6 o'clock sharp, Veerain is at my door. He is thrilled to bits. Docilely, and without showing much exuberance, I go to get into his car. I can see that my parents are still really uncertain about this decision of theirs.

But I don't think about anything. Yes, they are my parents, and they are expected to fret about everything. But this is the man I am going to marry in less than a month. If he can't be trusted with my protection and safety today, then how can my parents give me to him for my entire life?

Veerain begins driving. I am scared, and excited too. What if I am not supposed to go to Veerain's place like this before our wedding? Anything can happen tomorrow. But how do I make them understand that it would be impossible for me to step back now? I love him. I can't imagine my life without him now.

"What are you thinking?" Veerain asks me, blushingly. Something is definitely cooking in his mind. Something saucy. That is why he is going so red.

"Nothing as such. But why are you blushing? What is cooking in your head?" I ask straightaway.

He laughs. "You are going to stay at my place. I am just excited. I had never thought that I would get so attached to a girl one day, that it would cause me to wait so desperately for my wedding. I am so happy to have you in my life, Naina." He kisses my hand.

Who can stop oneself from falling in love, when one's fiancé is so adorable? I was having the exact same thoughts at home earlier in the afternoon.

He kisses my hand many more times before we reach his home, where I find his mom waiting to welcome me very warm-heartedly. She's even got a rangoli made on the porch, at their main door. She is an admirable lady – very coherent and genial. I am incredibly lucky to have her as my mom-in-law.

She has a special dinner cooked for me. Now I cannot wait to become a part of this family. I am falling in love with her, too. And I am totally overwhelmed with emotions right now. She cares for me. Veerain loves me. My life seems complete.

The three of us sit together for dinner in the dining area. As expected, she starts telling me about Veerain's nature, habits and childhood capers. We all laugh. And the food is really delicious. It is cooked simply, with light spices, but still tastes amazing. There is so much to learn from her. And I am so impressed with her that I want to become like her.

Veerain feels comfortable with her. There is no complaint, or frustration or anger for her in his heart. He rather seems very concerned. And why not? She is his mother, his everything. Seeing all this, I want to take care of her, just like Veerain does. After all, I have got love and happiness in my life because of her.

She chose me. She brought Veerain into my life. She is the reason for my happiness. She could have brought in a girl from any high society family. But she chose me. Thinking about this, I make a promise to myself that I will never disappoint her.

After dinner, she quietly gets up, and asks Veerain to wake her up before leaving the house. She even wishes me a good night adoringly, and then goes to her room.

Is she leaving Veerain and me alone now? It is just 9 o'clock! We have seven hours before Veerain leaves the house.

Right after she is gone, Veerain beckons me to accompany him to his room. He gets blissful. I follow him to his room. He is dancing on his way, shaking his hips. I guffaw.

Once we're inside, he closes the door immediately. What has gotten into him? I find my bag in his room. So, Aunty already had this plan to let us spend the night together. She is so cool!

Veerain climbs on his bed and starts dancing. He plays 'My House' by Flo Rida on his JBL Pulse 4 speaker. I didn't know he was a music lover. He is so much like me – like my twin soul. He switches off the light, but there is still enough light in the room to see. His speaker has a light show and it feels like a night club.

He makes me climb onto his bed as well. He is bouncing and lip-syncing the lyrics and rapping on the song. We both rap together, and dance like we are at a party on a beach. He plays all kinds of dope songs. I didn't know he was this fun. I see a child in him tonight – a kid who wants to enjoy life with his friends, who wants to have a chill time. I remember his breakdown over our call. He said that he doesn't usually get time for himself. When he is surrounded with his work, he is all engulfed in it. He doesn't remember to eat, drink, or take a break.

His face is looking so childlike right now, so naïve and innocent. He has his guard down.

"Hey, are you not enjoying yourself? Please, don't be a spoilsport," he grouches cutely.

I've got to trust him and stop crowding my head with negative thoughts. He turns the volume up, as 'Cheap Thrills' starts rolling.

I suddenly have an idea. And it may seem very schmaltzy, but I want to give it a try. I give some rest to Sia, as she has to hit the dance floor.

"What're you doing?" Veerain gripes.

"This may sound like a Disney song," I say, "but focus on the lyrics."

I play the song 'Until Forever' by Sarah Geronimo. Even Tanvi started to like it, after a while. Ruby and I used to listen to it whenever we were sad and hopeless about our love lives, and wanted to cry a little.

The background music starts rolling. And he is waiting for the lyrics. My heart is throbbing, and subconsciously, I am digging my nails into my palms.

After listening to the first two stanzas, patiently, he climbs down the bed and pulls me closer to him. He places his hands on my waist, I let mine dangle over his shoulders, and we swing with the tune.

When the main chorus comes, and the room fills with Sarah's loud melodious voice, he kisses me. It feels like I am in a Disney palace with my prince. He makes me feel like a princess. It is a dream come true. My heart confesses to me that I love him, only him.

I trust you, Veerain, even with myself.

We both lie back in his bed, and I get the inkling that he is planning to fall asleep now. It is going to strike eleven. We have five hours before he leaves. I don't want these five hours to slip away from my hands.

I take my bag and go to the washroom. I wear my net-nighty-gown with a G-string panty. It is completely sheer. I felt horribly shy when I had worn it for the first time and shown it to Ruby. She said it was so sexy that it turned her on. I know it will definitely knock out Veerain. But am I sure about it? Stop it, Naina. How much are you going to contemplate?

I hope he hasn't fallen asleep. I step outside. He is lying with his arm over his forehead. "Veerain," I say, timidly.

He looks at me. I feel the adrenaline rush in my body. He gawps at me for what feels like five minutes. He doesn't say anything. He is stupefied. I realise that the bathroom light is illuminating my naked body, and I get so nervous, I switch it off immediately.

Tonight knows no limits, restraint or self-control. We can't stay away from each other anymore. We become one. We feel united. As if we were one body, split up aeons and aeons ago, only to reunite tonight. It feels so right. And when John Legend is singing in his mellifluent voice in the background, 'Give your all to me, I'll give my all to you', how can one resist? It is not about pleasure. It is about having all of him.

I know how an orgasm feels. I have woken up with one from my spooky dreams with Raghav. But this is about love. It is so much deeper than any meaningless coitus. Now I learn the meaning of true love. When he is inside me, his gaze is adding the fire to the thrill his knob is diffusing in my body.

I never looked at Raghav this way in my dreams. His touch had always been full of lust, whereas now, I can feel pure love.

Love mixed with pleasure is the most powerful drug.

18

Shit!! He's late. I help him get ready, and we move in a hurry. We didn't sleep for a minute. He said he would sleep on the flight.

"Come on, Veerain, get into your pants." I tie the buttons of his shirt while he works to comb his hair. We were in his jacuzzi for an hour.

He is now ready to leave, but I can't go out like this. And I am not feeling like letting him go. I want to keep him clenched to my heart. He kisses me on the forehead and bids me goodbye. My body is trembling. My lips are quivering. I feel scared again, very scared. I quickly take a suit out of my bag, donning it. I go to the balcony and wait for him.

He comes out, but doesn't look up. "Veerain," I call out his name intrepidly. He looks back at me. My breath is cold. I feel the shiver in my body, but his gaze warms my heart. He gets into his car and drives off. I watch his car until it vanishes into the darkness.

I have never felt more scared before. Tears wet my cheeks. I love him, god. Please take care of him. I can't live without him.

I go down quietly to the temple inside their home, and sit in front of the picture of Lord Shiva with his family. I join my hands and feel warm tears cascading down. I get a snotty nose. But I sit like this until my body is calm, until I feel strong and confident again – until my heart says that he is going to be okay, and that he will return to me just as he has gone.

In the morning, when Aunty comes out, I have already made her breakfast. Chhotu had told me what she eats for breakfast. In fact, he'd told me about all Aunty's and Veerain's favourite dishes. He had gotten frightened to see me in the kitchen early in the morning. I was actually famished. I hadn't slept for a minute last night. Also, I burned a hell lot of calories, so I was looking for something to gobble in the morning.

Aunty gets stunned, as she enters the temple, to find that I have already lit the lamps and done the morning rituals. She smiles at me. She joins her hands and bows in the temple, then comes to the table for breakfast.

"I am impressed, Naina. You didn't sleep after Veerain left for the airport?" she asks caringly. I do not say anything; just serve her food.

"You made this, semolina omelette?" she asks me.

"Yeah," I say docilely. I'd sampled a morsel of it, and it had tasted fine to me.

"It is nice," I hear her say. She smiles gently.

We talk about random stuff. She tells me that there is a pooja in their ancestral temple, so she will go there with Chhotu. He helps in serving *prasad* to the visitors.

"What will you do at home?" she asks me.

"I can come with you," I suggest politely.

"No, I don't want people to see you this soon. You will catch evil eyes. I don't even take Veerain with me to the temple. I ask him to go to some other temple, if he wishes to. People don't appreciate you much nowadays. They sadden to see you thriving." She is absolutely right, and totally unlike my parents. They, rather, force me and Bhaiya to attend such events at the temple against our will.

I roam the house with her for a while, and she tells me about their relatives and their respective natures. She also talks about Raghav and Veerain's aversion to each other. She shares how much this upsets her. After Veerain's father had passed away, his Tauji had looked after Veerain. She had never wanted Veerain and Raghav to fight like animals. She tells me about their recent separation from Tauji's family and business, because of the stupid tussle between Raghav and Veerain. Also that Veerain doesn't listen to her, in the matter of Raghav. He hadn't invited Raghav to the engagement – but still, Raghav had shown true gentlemanship and brotherhood by coming to the function. This is what she thinks.

Shit! She has such a wrong perception of Raghav. Oh! She is so far away from reality. Hasn't she noticed once the frustration and anger that Veerain has smothered for Raghav?

Parents will be parents, however cool they might be. I wonder, what will be her reaction when she learns about Raghav's and Veerain's enmity because of me?

She and Chhotu leave for the temple. I am missing Veerain. And this empty house is making me miss him even more. His flight will land around 11:30 a.m. It is 11 o'clock right now. Soon, I will hear his voice, but of course, he can't chitchat. He has a meeting at 2 o'clock.

I get comfortable on the couch. I want to sleep, but I can't stop reminiscing over the memory of last night. Veerain said he would never forget the night, never in his life. It had been the best night of his life.

He doesn't know yet that there will be many more such moments to cherish in the future. He is my life, and I want to make him feel special, always.

I see Raghav walking in from the main door. What is he doing in here? My heartbeat increases. I get to my feet.

He chuckles at me. "Hey, Naina! How are you doing?" he asks.

I don't say anything. Veerain's flight would not have landed yet. I can't call Aunty or anyone else.

"Not happy to see me?" he grins. "I am ecstatic. I missed you so much, darling."

"Are you a psycho? What are you doing here?" I squawk, anxiously.

"Always so hyper! Since you met that bastard, you are always so peevish. He doesn't take good care of you?! I don't get what you see in him." He comes too close to me. I take a step back. But he comes closer. I move back and he steps forward.

"Stop it, Raghav. I'll call Aunty. Leave now," I threaten him feebly. My heart is pounding hard and my legs have gone numb.

"Leave? I am here to take you, Naina." He chuckles.

"Take me?" I feel a prickling sensation in my entire body.

"Yes, today, we are getting married," Raghav laughs. Madness has completely swept over him. I sprint to the stairs to my left, to lock myself in Veerain's room.

But he gets hold of me. He grips my hand and brings me down.

"Raghav, why are you doing all this? You know that I don't love you," I mutter.

He pulls me close, holds me from behind. I break into a cold sweat. He wraps his hands around my belly and smells my hair. I fidget. What shall I do? Nobody except Veerain could even think that he took me away. And Veerain is far away.

"I love you. Finally, we can be together. Everyone will accept you as their daughter-in-law, once they learn how Veerain played his ugly game on us," he mumbles. He brings his lips close to my left cheek. I swiftly turn my face to the right, hitting him in his chest with my elbow. But his grip is too tight.

"Come on, Naina. Don't be so hard on yourself. You're thinking I am pushing myself on you?! That only I want you in my life."

What shall I do? I don't want to marry him. He is demented. My breath has grown warm now, and my lips have dried out.

"After our wedding," he says, "I'll take you to a brilliant doctor in the U.S. She will help you to learn the truth about our love. Don't worry. You have nothing to fret about. I am there for you. I'll never treat you like that bastard does. I am not angry at you. I know you don't know anything yet."

How do I run? I can't find a way. Where is my phone?

He swings me around abruptly. I try to push him away from me. But as much as I am trying to push him away, he is coming closer. I can't stop him. He laughs. I feel his breath over my nose. I think I'm going to faint.

"Honey, you love me. It is just that you don't know it yet." I hear his words. Then, his lips start rotating. I think my head is spinning. I see him coming closer. I shut my eyes.

He kisses me.

"Raghav!"

I open my eyes at the shrill voice. Raghav lets go of me and steps back. I see fear on his face. I look at the gate.

It is Veerain's mom. I go rushing to her. Her eyes are red. She is burning with indignation. I think of telling her about Raghav's plan, but she slaps me so hard that it hurts my jaw. I stand astonished. She goes to Raghav.

"She is an outsider. But you are Veerain's brother. How could you do this? They are going to be married in a month, Raghav!" she yells thunderously.

He stands with a hangdog face. He doesn't know what to say. Tears fall down my cheeks.

"Veerain loves her." She shakes Raghav to speak, then looks at me. "I shouldn't have thought of bringing a low-class girl into my family in the first place. You are a loose woman – a cheap woman, who can sleep with anyone. Last night you slept with my son. And today..." She spits on the floor.

"Aunty, I am sorry. I shouldn't have come here," Raghav says apologetically to her. I look at him in wonder. Pretending to be all innocent, he leaves.

"Leave, right now! I can't tolerate your ugly face," Aunty growls at me. "Take your bag and leave!" Tears wet my cheeks.

Raghav has ruined everything for me. He's wrecked my life.

"My son loves you so much that he called me to go home and check on you. You were not picking up his phone calls, so he got worried. And here, you were getting ready to sleep with his brother," she splutters.

"No, no, no Aunty. You are taking it all wrong. He came here to drag me out of the house to marry him forcefully." I blurt out.

"Why would he do that?" she asks sternly.

"I met him three months ago. He saw me with my friends, and since then, he has been chasing me. I didn't know he was Veerain's brother. I came to know when I saw him on our engagement day," I cry.

"Why would any boy from a respectable family go mad for you? Why would he chase you like that? I saw you at that wedding looking at my son. I saw Veerain noticing you too. For the sake of Veerain's happiness, I approached your family. I thought that you were not like today's girls. You don't take pleasure in influencing young boys to get mad for you. But you are no different. You are shameless, have zero values, and no regard for others' feelings. Under my roof, behind my son and me, you were planning to sleep with his brother." She spits venom for me. My ears are about to bleed.

"Please, stop it, Aunty. You know nothing. Ask your son. He knows everything. He will understand why Raghav came here. Veerain will listen and trust me, because he knows the truth. He knows everything." I cry. "I am not going anywhere until Veerain comes," I tell her clearly.

"Veerain knows what?" she screams, acridly. "He will not marry a cheap woman like you. I will not let my son marry a loose woman. He is under your charm right now, but he loves me, and he will believe what I saw."

She is not understanding the truth behind what she just saw. "What you saw is not true!" I holler. "It is a misunderstanding. I was not kissing him. He had clenched me and wasn't letting me go. He wanted to force himself on me. I am not a loose woman. If I am a loose woman, then every girl in this world is. Every single girl!" I am a girl with respect. I deserve to be respected.

My head is going to explode with pain. I pour myself some water and sit on the couch.

She calls Veerain. She screams so horribly on the phone that I get the jitters. She asks Veerain to catch the first flight available, and come back to India. After disconnecting the call, she looks at me fiercely, like she wants to flay the skin off my bones, then goes to her room.

I get Veerain's call. Picking it up, I dash to his room. Hearing his voice melts my heart. Tears spring in my eyes, and I start crying. He asks me what happened, but my heart is pounding so crazily that I can't speak a word. How do I tell him that his mom thinks I am a slut? The hurt of Aunty's comments is what's killing me.

He consoles me. He tells me exactly what my heart needs to hear. He says he is there for me, and that he will make everything right when he comes back. That nothing has changed. He says that he loves me, and will not forgive Raghav for what he did. I open up now and, like a baby, I narrate to him everything that happened. He asks me to stay strong, and says that he will come home tonight. Till then, I do not try to mollify Aunty, but do make sure that she eats something. He knows her nature. He will take care of her. This calms me down.

At the end of our call, he goes for his meeting. I lie down in his bed, mentally and physically exhausted.

After waking up, I spend my day in the drawing room. Aunty doesn't come out of her room. I tell Chhotu what to cook and ask him to serve lunch to Aunty in her room.

Later, he comes and tells me that she is refusing to eat. Now, she is behaving just like my parents. I take a cup of coffee with an apple and a painkiller for my crushing headache.

Chhotu asks me if something happened between Aunty and me. I think, he believes that we fought while he was at the ancestral temple. I do not say anything... just gesture a 'no'.

I wait around like this on the couch till eleven in the night for Veerain to arrive. His flight has landed. He should reach home in twenty minutes.

I ask Chhotu to sleep, and in the meantime, I warm up food for Veerain and Aunty, as she has not eaten anything since breakfast. She hasn't left her room since then, either.

She is more stern and stubborn than my mother, it seems. My mom would have eaten by now, and pretended like she was starving, no less. In that case, it is still easy to handle the person. Here, Aunty's blood pressure would have lowered. And due to hypertension, she would be more cranky and feeble too. How does one deal with such a person, other than accepting what they want?

I am scared to bits. I do not care about Raghav, nor do I want to teach him a lesson. I just want to convince Aunty that I am not the type of girl she now thinks I am. And only Veerain can convince her.

Hearing a car pulling up outside, I rush to the main door, but do not open it. What if it is Raghav again? The dreadful thought sends chills down my spine. My phone rings in the kitchen. It would be Veerain.

I open the door. It is Veerain. I hug him tightly in the doorway.

"It is okay, baby. I am here now." His words calm me down.

"Veerain." An angry growl comes from behind me. It is Veerain's mom. She doesn't look weak; rather, she looks sturdy and ready for a fight. It makes me swallow the thick lump in me down.

And right there, she starts with all the allegations, and there is defiance in her tone. Like she has made up her mind for something, and in no way is she going to change it, whereas Veerain looks sick. He is very tired. Obviously, he would be. He didn't sleep last night. And then today, he travelled to another country and then came all the way back.

Very calmly, though, he makes Aunty sit, then gives her some water to drink. He asks me to bring the food for her. But she refuses to eat anything.

Next, he asks me to bring the medicine from his room. He is feeling sick. I go hurriedly to his room. I don't know what will happen. What if Veerein isn't able to convince Aunty?

When I come back, I see Aunty placing food on the dining table for Veerain. I stop near the couch. I should stay out of it, and give them their own time. It is me she is furious at, not Veerain.

Veerain feeds Aunty with his own hand. That is adorable. Am I coming between the mother and son? But I never wanted that. I wanted to care for Aunty, just like Veerain does. I have revered her ever since I first saw her. I wanted her to like me, not hate me. I will never be able to forget this day in my life, nor will I be able to forget her hatred for me. I don't know if I'll ever be able to win her heart back.

She orders Veerain to call my brother and ask him to pick me up from here. I stand up in astonishment. My heart jumps into my mouth. She looks at me, but Veerain doesn't.

"Why are you saying so, Mom?" he asks her calmly, and continues eating his food.

"You are asking me the reason? Didn't I tell you enough?" She gets into a stew.

"Mom, I trust you. I believe you. I love you. And you know that. I need you to trust me, too. It is not Naina who is at fault. You remember that I didn't want to marry this soon. But you forced me to meet the girl at least." He holds her hand.

"Yeah, that was my mistake," she grumbles.

"Mom, at least hear me out first, then give your verdict. Don't you want the best for me? Don't you want to see me happy? When I met her, I liked her, but I still didn't want to marry so soon. At that time, she told me about another guy who was after her. And he had even threatened her that he would not let anyone else marry her. I asked to see the picture of that guy. That guy was Raghav. I wasn't shocked, because I always knew he was a scallywag. You don't believe he is, in spite of the truth being in front of your eyes."

Her eyes widen. She looks staggered. I can see she wants to say something, but Veerain stops her.

"Yes," he continues, "I knew it since our first meeting that Raghav was after Naina. Mom, you liked her. Everyone liked her. Even I liked her. She captivated me so much that I was forced to think over about my decision. And just because Raghav was fixated on her, I should have stayed out of it and let a wonderful lady go away from my life? No. It was because of our fate that our cars collided, and you saw her again. It was our fate which brought Naina and me together. And then, when he saw her at the engagement, you know how he is. He got vindictive and abusive. I had to block him on my phone to avoid any further wrangle. But Mom, he crossed all limits today. After today, I can't trust him with Naina. He entered our home and assaulted your daughter-in-law." Veerain's tone changes. He gets indignant.

"What will you do?" Aunty speaks sulkily. "You will go to his house and beat the shit out of him? You will beat your brother for a girl?"

"How can you say that? After all that he did today? He came to our house to forcefully take Naina away. What if you hadn't come back in time, and he had raped her? Would you have said the same thing, then? 'Fight with your brother for the sake of a girl?' Mom, what about the principles you taught me? About respecting every woman? Did he show brotherhood by putting a hand on his sister-in-law? And you are talking about brotherhood. Mom, I am going to Tauji and Taiji's house right now. I will tell them that I am going to file an FIR against Raghav for sexually assaulting my fiancée in my house," Veerain says incandescently. This shakes me up. I get to my feet again.

"Veerain, no!" Aunty screeches.

But Veerain gets up. "I am going right now with Naina!" he says. "She has Raghav's WhatsApp messages. I'll show them that he has been torturing her. I also have Raghav's messages abusing me, threatening to give me a good lesson that I would never forget in my life. He even texted me that he would kill me."

"Veerain, beta, please stop it. I have only you. I wanted to bring happiness into my family through a daughter-in-law, and not this upheaval and animosity between brothers," she cries. I feel sad and ashamed that all this is happening because of me.

"No, Mom. You forgot that I love this girl. I can't let go of a scoundrel who misbehaved with the woman I love. This is why I left Naina at our home, under your protection. I never had faith in Raghav. I knew he could stoop to any level. He is a guttersnipe. He needs to be shown his real place. Today, Mom, if you stop me, you will lose your son."

"Calm down, Veerain!" I shout from the back. He has said enough in my support.

"Aunty, I am not the type of girl you think I am," I say, turning to her. "But I am ashamed of myself now, for bringing this tumult instead of happiness into this family. And I don't know what to do now, to change or stop it. And I swear on my love for Veerain that I do not have any illicit relation with Raghav. Raghav was forcefully trying to touch me. And I didn't encourage him. I've never had a boy in my life, before your son. He is my first and last," I whimper.

"C'mon, Naina. We are going to Tauji's place. Get your cell phone," Veerain says to me. I don't think it is a good idea. This matter will become huge, and we don't know how they will react to it. After all, Raghav is their son.

"No, Veerain," I reply. "It is late right now. They would have gone to sleep. We can go in the morning." I think, until morning, his anger will dwindle down.

"No," he says sternly, raising me on pins and needles. "It is a grave matter, and it needs an alarming action. We are leaving now," he refuses to listen.

"I'll come along," Aunty says grimly. It gives me some relief, even though she is not on my side. But still she can handle Veerain, and speak in-between, to control the situation.

It is all dark outside. I am quivering with fear and cold. It is a quarter to one. I am not getting a good feeling about all this.

In the car, Aunty sits next to Veerain in the front. I sit in the back. No one talks in the car. The roads are abandoned and dark.

We reach Raghav's house, and my heart is pounding heavily. All the lights are off. They are surely asleep at this hour. Why are we doing this? I am feeling so guilty for bringing the matter to this point, in spite of no mistake of mine. It was Raghav who came to drag me out of the house and marry me against my will. Would he have literally married me forcefully today? The thought alone sends me into shudders.

Veerain is calling somebody on his phone. I think they didn't pick up his call. So, he calls again. I want to ask him to stop, but I don't think he will listen. Tonight, he showed tremendous faith in me. I can't disappoint him now.

He finally speaks to someone on the phone. I think that's his Tauji. I can't really ask him. I am too scared of his reaction. He is looking calm from outside... but inside, I know he is seething with anger.

After a little wait, somebody opens the door. It's his Taiji. Veerain touches her feet. She looks frightened to see all of us together like this. Maybe she had only expected to see Veerain. She asks fretfully what has happened, and Veerain's mom answers that Veerain will tell her.

My heart is thumping in my chest. I am feeling guilty. And I don't know why. I am not scared of Veerain's Tauji's and Taiji's reactions, that what would they think of me? I am fearing that they don't ask Veerain to either call off the wedding with me, or to cut off all ties with their family.

Shit! I am screwed. Veerain's Tauji comes hurriedly with a solicitous expression.

I am the cause of all of this. But am I, really? Why do I lust for Raghav in my dreams? Do I have feelings for him?

Veerain, without beating around the bush, tells them everything. And they, with each and every revelation, look at me like I am the reason for it.

Veerain's Taiji looks at me despicably, then refuses to believe all of this.

She stands up in denial. Tauji asks Taiji to call Raghav, and direct him come to home right now. She pulls out her phone to call, while muttering things about me – saying that it would be stupid of them to doubt their boy, for the sake of some girl they don't even know well.

Nobody stops her. And tears begin to spring in my eyes. No, I don't expect Veerain to misbehave with her. But still, it hurts. I am feeling like a real culprit now.

We all sit in dead silence. I am shuddering. Taiji is glaring at me scornfully, but I keep my eyes downcast. Tauji, conversely, is perched with his eyes closed and his head lowered. There is a great strain on his forehead. My hands have gotten sweaty and my mouth has gone dry. I want water. I didn't even have lunch or dinner today. How will I face Raghav? My heartbeat increases, and I feel like swooning. I pass out on the couch.

Coming to, I hear a rustle of motion and voices. They all are hovering over me. Veerain is checking my blood pressure. Veerain's mom is standing next to him with a glass of water in her hand. Even Tauji is showing concern for me, and asks me to lie down in the guestroom.

Taiji is seated fussily. She mumbles, "Why is she so scared? What is she scared of?" She wants to say that I am afraid of getting busted, as her heroic son is about to come and put an end to all their doubts. I scoff. Her saintly son doesn't even live with her. He is in the same city, and still lives in his own apartment. Just compare him to Veerain. Veerain is so responsible. He takes care of his mother, and is attentive towards his duties. That is the kind of son every mother wishes for. That's why this woman is so jealous of Veerain.

I see Raghav walking in. It gives me a fresh, cold shudder. His image of kissing me today looms in my head.

He has no hint of shame on his face. Instead, he looks surly. Veerain's Tauji gets up immediately, without wasting a moment. He asks Raghav in an angry and clear tone, did he visit their house today or not? Very calmly, Raghav nods that he did. He is acting so cool and serene about this. Then, Tauji asks him if he met me today in the house – to which Raghav again nods. Tauji asks him why he had gone there, because, as far as he knows him, that is the last place he would wish to go to. To this question, Raghav doesn't reply. Tauji shouts at him so thunderously that it shakes me like a leaf. Raghav's face distorts with indignation, but he keeps his head down.

Taiji intervenes, stepping between them.

"Why are you shouting at your son in front of outsiders? He is your son. When will you start trusting him?" Taiji bellows at Tauji. I have never seen my mother talking to my dad in this tone. This family is sick.

"Tell them, Raghav, why did you go to that house?" Taiji asks him. "My son has studied in the US. He has dated models. He has independently started his liquor business, and opened night clubs in Delhi. My son would never stoop to that level, that too for a girl like her. She is the one trying to lure him. It is clear. Look at her, and look at our son. Kavita, I am telling you, don't make this mistake of bringing a low-class wench into our family." Taiji spits filth for me. How many times am I going to be humiliated today!

She starts dissing me again, "You, trollop. Why don't you tell the truth to everyone? Your plan has floundered. You wanted to seduce my son; you called him to the house." She attacks me mercilessly, and I start crying right there.

"Mom, stop it! How can you harass her like that?" I hear Raghav erupt in anger and his mother stares at him in disbelief. "Yes, harass her. I went to their house to talk to her, because I love her. I have loved her long before Veerain came into the picture. We both went on a date and I even proposed to her to marry me. And this filthy, favourite son of yours, Dad – he took my girlfriend away from me. Naina was about to say yes to me, pretty soon. But this cuss came in between us."

I feel my soul departing my body. Girlfriend? Is he really this demented.

"Raghav, don't do this," Veerain's Taiji says to him. "I have supported you every single time. Don't throw away our faith in you for this strumpet."

Veerain and Raghav, together, object to her dissing me like this. Veerain finally speaks up in my honour. "Don't use ill words for our daughter-in-law. Don't forget that she is Veerain's fiancée," Tauji gripes too, to Taiji for me.

"Naina, was there anything between you and Raghav before this engagement?" Tauji asks me earnestly.

I get scared. What do I say? "No, Tauji," Veerain interjects. "When I met Naina, she told me about a boy who was harassing her. That guy was forcing her to marry him, in spite of her telling him, distinctly, that she had no interest in him. I really liked Naina's honesty and simplicity. That's why I said yes to her. I asked her to block that guy, and she did. Then, on our engagement day, I found out that it was Raghav who was after her. I could not believe it myself. Even Naina was staggered to learn that he was my brother.

"I tried to talk to Raghav about this, and clear the mist. I texted him. See, Tauji, here is our last conversation."

Veerain shows his mobile chat to Tauji.

"Raghav, in his rage, completely forgot that he was talking to his brother. He threatened to kill me. Not just this, Tauji, he even halted Naina's car on the way to my office, and forcefully barged into her car to threaten her to cancel this wedding. He is losing more and more control of himself, day by day. And today's incident was the last straw. I can't trust him with Naina now. He has no shame for his bhabhi. Despite his feelings for her in the past, he should understand that she is his bhabhi now, and that she never felt for him the way she does for me."

I can't believe Veerain. How smartly he concocted the whole story of him being as innocent as I am!

But his words fiercely enrage Raghav. He holds Veerain by his collar. We all panic and shoot up to stop them. Tauji steps in, separating them, while Aunty holds on to Veerain's arm and pulls him back. Veerain's Taiji clenches Raghav tightly.

"Enough," Tauji bawls. "Raghav, I've had enough of your behaviour. Is this why we sent you to a foreign university, to become a beast? I have borne all of your unreasonable and extravagant expenses and pursuits. I have never said a word in disapproval of your lifestyle, which I've in fact never liked. Because I always had a hope that you would change, eventually. You would become responsible, and begin understanding your duties toward this family. But tonight, I think you have crossed all limits. I disown you. I throw you out of my family and my business. I cut all my ties with you. I take my name back from you. From now on, you are not my son and legal heir of my property." Tauji's voice wobbles, speaking the last sentences. He is shattered.

Raghav is petrified too. His eyes go bloodshot. I feel bad for him. Is it fair? He genuinely loves me. I was not going to say 'yes' to him, but Veerain did involve himself in it, only to get back at Raghav – though Veerain loves me now. I really don't know who is more at fault in this. Maybe Raghav, for not stepping back and pointlessly obsessing over me?

Raghav leaves quietly.

We all stay seated silently, locked in a daze at what has happened. Taiji is in her room, sobbing. Tauji asks Veerain to quicken the wedding arrangements. Also, he apologises to us for Raghav's behaviour. After sitting there for some time, we leave.

In the car, Aunty scolds Veerain for creating this chaos. She says that Veerain is just as much at fault here as Raghav. Veerain had riled Raghav to react in that way. He should have never said 'yes' to this marriage. She says she doesn't believe me, either, about not knowing about Raghav's relation to Veerain.

While stepping outside the car, she tells Veerain that she regrets her decision of bringing me into this family. I took her son away from her. I taught her son to lie to his mother, to whom he had never lied before. Veerain lied to his fatherly Tauji about his knowledge of Raghav pursuing me. He broke the relation between father and son today, all for me. She says Veerain is not her same old son anymore.

Part – 2

In the present…

19

"Hello? Ruby? Please, I need you. I'll die... please come to meet me," I sob into the phone.

"Are you okay? Naina, what happened?" Ruby panics.

"I have no idea what is happening to me. I am turning mad," I explode over the phone.

"Relax, baby! Come on, breathe in, and breathe out. Everything is going to be fine."

She's trying to calm me. She is not getting it. I have tried a lot of ways to calm myself down already. But nothing is working.

"I need to see a psychiatrist. I am losing my mind!" I howl.

"Baby, I spoke with you a week ago when you came back from your honeymoon. You were so happy. What has happened in a week?" Ruby asks.

"I lied!" I break down. I snivel.

"Lied about what? Veerain? Did he do something?" She's getting alarmed.

"No, no. It is not Veerain. It is me. And it started long back – even before we had gotten married. I had thought that it would stop. But it didn't. It only grew stronger. I didn't tell you guys about it. I was ashamed of myself. And now, it has gotten out of my control.

It is overpowering me now. I am scared that Veerain will hear his name out of my mouth one night, and then he will leave me forever. I love him, Ruby. I love him," I blubber.

"What are you talking about? Whose name?" she cries.

"Raghav's. I say Raghav's name in my dreams. I am scared that Veerain will hear me saying his name in my dream, and then, he will abandon me. I love Veerain. I can't live without him. And Raghav is not letting me live with him," I whimper.

"You are scaring me, Naina. Why do you take Raghav's name in your dreams? What do you have to do with him? You haven't seen him for a month, even more than that." Ruby asks.

How do I explain this to her? "Please, book me an appointment with Dr Sujata, the one you took your cousin to," I implore her.

"My cousin was stupid, just like you. That doctor refused to see her after her second appointment. And she is going to do the same with you, because you are absolutely fine. You are just acting crazy."

"You are not getting it," I say. "Come pick me up, now, please."

Ruby comes to pick me up and suggests we go to a restaurant and talk, but I insist on sitting in her car.

She is perplexed. I don't even know where to start. I begin by telling her about my first dream, which I had had two-and-a-half months ago. These dreams began after meeting Raghav. I tell her that initially, they were infrequent; they came once every fifteen days or so. Then, they started coming once a week. And soon after, two-three times a week. And after my wedding, on my honeymoon, they began to grow more frequent. For two weeks now, I have consistently been experiencing the same dream of Raghav and me together. There is an enormous pond and snakes. Earlier, there hadn't been snakes, but now they are there. I feel scared and horribly frightened. I know that I sound unhinged, but all this is true. She asks me, how had Veerain not noticed this madness in me? I tell her what I have told Veerain that I have turned into an insomniac.

"I purposefully do not sleep. I drink black coffee right before going to bed. Because when Veerain and I would have finished, we would lay down to sleep, and in my dream, I would see myself with Raghav. He, like a snake, would be crawling all over my body," I heave.

"Oh dear god!" she says. "You see yourself with Raghav every night in your dreams, getting shagged. Does he metamorphose into a snake as well?"

"No, no. He doesn't," I gasp, "but that place is full of snakes. It is a cavern. It is completely dark. Mashals are flaring on the mud walls. Raghav looks like Raghav, just in weird clothes, and most of the time, without them. I haven't seen myself wearing anything up till now, except for bangles. I am wearing heavy gold bangles. My wrists disappear in them."

"Why are you getting such creepy dreams? You look and sound like a crackpot," she shrieks at me in concern as I sob.

"Don't cry, baby. I will not leave you alone in this mess. I know you can't talk to Veerain about this. I'll talk to the doctor and try to get an appointment for you soon." Ruby hugs me tightly. I feel safe and secure. She will take care of everything.

"You know what, Ru? What kills me more? That I sleep with Veerain and dream of Raghav. I am just done with Veerain and then Raghav takes over me," I speak throatily.

"Shhh! Quiet. These are only bad dreams. Nothing is happening in reality. They will soon vanish, once we start taking the treatment. Okay? And you don't have to tell anyone about this," Ruby replies, caressing my head. I embrace her tightly for some comfort.

20

Ruby picks me up today. She is driving calmly beside me. It will take an hour for us to reach the hospital. She has already spoken to the doctor about my case. I have checked Dr Sujata's profile on Google. She is MBBS and MD in psychiatry. She has fifteen years of experience. She will understand me, hopefully.

"How is your mother-in-law doing? Is she still surly with you?" asks Ruby.

"I don't care, honestly. She can stay like this forever if she wishes to. Because of that douche, she has been giving us a cold shoulder. Now, she has gotten soft with Veerain, but she's still apathetic towards me. Raghav has taken all my peace and happiness away. All the time, I am fidgeting," I drone.

"That's because you don't sleep. Dr Sujata told me it is because of the sleep deprivation," she says.

I have told Veerain that I am going to a doctor to talk about my sudden insomnia. He's asked me to tell him what the doctor says, when I told him that I was going to see Ruby's family doctor, and that he can help.

We wait for the doctor in her clinic. This room is filled with pictures of the brain and of nerves. These are basically diagrams, meant to help explain the internal functioning of our brain. But they are making me feel woozy.

I am not brainsick. Whatever I am, right now, it is all because of Raghav.

Dr Sujata comes in. She gives me a warm smile, and begins asking me about my health, and my relation with the people around me. She doesn't come to my dreams directly. I tell her everything very honestly and frankly. I tell her the entire story at length, and in detail.

Now, she asks me specifically about my dreams, and demands for me to be meticulous. I narrate every detail that I can remember. And I guess I am thorough with these dreams, as I see the same dream every night, with just slight variations.

"Could I say that you got scared of Raghav, when he threatened you about involving your parents?" Dr Sujata propounds.

"It infuriated me more. But yes," I answer. "In a way, I was also frightened that he would get my marriage cancelled, or find a way to create trouble for me."

"When did you get that weird dream, exactly, for the first time? Do you remember anything unusual happening with you, right before that dream?" she inquires.

I will really have to jog my memory for this. "Umm, yes. I don't know if that counts. But it was unusual for me, because that was my first ever kiss. Actually, a day before that dream came, Veerain kissed me. And that was my first ever kiss," I say timidly.

"So, that was your first time you got intimate with a boy," Dr Sujata repeats.

"Not intimate. Yeah, intimate. But then, I got intimate with Veerain, and I swear to god, I never thought of Raghav in that way. And the night I got that dream, I was actually fantasising about

Veerain and me, not about Raghav. So, why did he come in my dream?"

"You never imagined yourself with Raghav in such an intimate position and situation?" She's trying to dig out some unexpected fact.

"No," I say. "I never have. And as I have told you, I loathe myself for having such dreams. I want them to stop. They are having a bad impact on my life and my marriage. I feel that I'll soon turn insane."

"Okay, I get it." She becomes quiet. She starts looking at her notes pensively.

It's been half an hour since she's spoken a word. I look around her clinic to kill time. I see a picture on the wall, of her receiving an award by the American Association for Community Psychiatry.

I look back at her; she is absorbed in her computer screen after our three-hour session, whereas she had originally told me it would be a two-hour meeting. She will definitely find a solution for me.

I remember once Raghav had muttered to me, when he had come to abduct me at our house, that he would take me to a brilliant doctor in the US. Why did he say that?

"I think this is your case," she murmurs, still staring at her computer screen. Ruby and I get sharp-eyed.

"I have made your complete report, and notes of my observation and findings. I'll email this to you. You can read it and let me know if you are ready," she says.

"No, please, tell me now," I say.

"You need hypnotism. I usually do not recommend this. And it is not a valid practice in this hospital. But seeing your case, I think it is the only option. Hear me out first. What I have noticed in your case is that you strangely have every minute detail of these moments happening in your dream: the environment around you, the clothes you and he were wearing, the place you were in, the jewellery you were wearing, you can recall it all. And all of these dreams are quite the same. It seems like a continuation of one singular moment. And you have noticed the activities taking place in your dreams from so close, and have felt them as if they were real. Even though you have never been to that place and been this intimate with that boy, Raghav."

"So? What do you mean?" Ruby asks.

"I mean to say that, maybe, she had been there in her past. Her memory from the past is trying to come to light. Something is triggering those memories, and she thinks it is Raghav. Because only after meeting him, these hidden memories of her past have started to come out." Dr Sujata utterly fails to explain her point.

"What past?" I ask her, somewhat numbly.

"Your past. Something you don't remember clearly," she answers.

"You mean that these are not my dreams, but actual, real memories from my past. What past? I am twenty-four years old. And I am just about this young in my dreams. Then, which past of my life are you talking about?" I am starting to lose my mind now. I think I know the answer, but I don't want any kind of link or association with Raghav to be true. I have never been touched and fondled by Raghav in my life, and this is the only truth I want to live with.

"Relax and go home," I hear her say. "I am emailing you a link. When you are calm and your mind is clear, have a look at it. I am also prescribing you some medicines for deep sleep."

"No, I am not going anywhere. I have been reduced to a bundle of nerves. And whatever you have just said has only made it worse. I want you to explain everything in more detail, and openly."

I'd told her everything, and waited an hour for an answer – and this is what she is giving me?

Ruby caresses my shoulders and tells me that we have exceeded our session. That we should book another appointment now.

"No, no. I understand that. If you want to charge me for two sessions, that is fine, but please, help me out. I feel like I have been getting raped for two-and-a-half months, by a person I loathe more than anyone or anything in this world. I have started to loathe myself now. Please, I beg you!"

"Okay, calm down," the doctor says, popping out a pill from a strip and handing it over to me. "You are too stressed. Drink some water. Swill this pill with it." I swallow it with water.

"It is, maybe, from your past life. These memories could be from your previous birth," she continues. "It is a long theory. Just fathom this for now, that we all have many births. And we need to find out that which birth of yours is related to these fragments of your memory – and why they are trying to take hold of you. For this, I'll have to conduct hypnosis on you. It will let you see things lucidly, and we will try to extract some details about these dreams from your subconscious mind, which still contains details of your past life." She sounds eccentric to me.

21

I am really thankful to Ruby for supporting me. No one else knows that I am going for a hypnosis session today. I told Veerain and Mom that I'm going to stay at Ruby's tonight. Veerain had asked me why, but I had told him that it was just for old time's sake – a girly slumber party.

I don't know how I am going to feel after this session, whether I'll be in any condition to go home or not. So, I told them that after lunch, I'll go to Ruby's place.

I am really curious and nervous about this weird therapy. I have no idea what the result will be.

We reach Dr Sujata's personal clinic, which is located on the ground floor of her residence. My heartbeats quicken. Dr Sujata had said that the hospital doesn't support hypnotism, so she would conduct it at her personal clinic. She'd asked me to come with a full stomach, as the session could take three to four hours.

We enter. This place looks cool – pretty amazing, actually. It is designed like an activity club – colourful and vibrant. There are different types of chairs, sofas and recliners spaced around the area, accompanied by musical instruments like flutes, keyboard, drums, guitar, violin, cello, harmonica, trumpet and bells.

"Why so many musical instruments?" I ask Dr Sujata, while she is lighting incense sticks, the fragrance of which invigorates me.

"Do you play any instruments?" she asks me warmly.

"No," I respond meekly. I am a talentless person that way.

"I have a karaoke system too, if you like to sing," she suggests.

"Oh, that makes me feel like a total loser who is good at nothing," I say.

"All of this is actually for people who think exactly like you. So, we will have fun some other day. Today, you have to come to this room." She holds open a door to a room – a cabin, in fact. There is a recliner, and a rocking chair opposite it.

"You know where to sit," she says to me.

I spread-eagle onto the upholstered recliner. There is no extra chair for Ruby.

"Ruby," Dr Sujata says, "you can bring in any light chair from outside, and perch behind Naina. Keep a little distance from her recliner."

"Naina, here, drink some water. And it has a drug mixed into it. So, your head will get a little drowsy.

I take a small sip of it. It's a bit salty.

Dr Sujata disappears from the room, then comes back with a remote in her hand. "We are going to record this entire session. I'll switch off the lights, and then, this Hypnotise Spiral will start shining bright. You have to stare at the screen, and only at the screen, for fifteen minutes. I'll take over the session from there. Okay? Please, go to the loo before we begin with the process."

It seems like she has done this before, many times.

"I have a question. Is it dangerous, like, harmful to one's health?" I ask anxiously.

"Relax," she replies. "It is totally harmless. And I am certified to practice it. I have done this a hundred times before. I'm going to play some soothing music in the background – like this." She turns on a pleasant piece of music.

"You will keep your focus on the screen," she says. There is a digital screen on the wall, right in front of me, with an optical illusion of spirals on its surface.

"You will slowly feel relaxed, and feel your head getting heavy. You will want to shut your eyes, but you will not. You will keep staring at the screen, until I ask you to close your eyes. Slowly, your mind will grow hyperactive. You will not get sleepy; rather, your mind will become super active. Your eyes will then be closed, and you will follow my instructions. I'll ask you to search within your subconscious mind. It will be like searching for a file on your desktop. Your eyes will be closed, and you will be able to see the memories we are doing all this to find. But it will take time to make you see them. That is my job. Don't be scared. You will be aware of everything happening in this room. I am just, with the help of drugs, making you unleash the power of your mind. Okay? Now relax."

Relax? I am so nervous. My heart is pounding and I am cold.

I go to the washroom and try to calm myself. Oh! My hands are cold, and my head is swirling. Her drug is working already.

"Naina, are you okay? Come out fast. She is calling you!" Ruby blares outside the door. I step out.

She makes me lie on the recliner, and also gives me a blanket to keep me warm. The room is dark now, and only the optical illusion screen is illuminated. My head starts swirling really fast, seeing the twirling spirals. I shut my eyes.

"No, Naina, focus! It will take you almost half an hour to get ready for the next step." I hear her voice. I am feeling pukish, and my head is heavy, like I drank too much inebriant. Still, I stare at the screen with complete focus.

"Tell me, Naina, how are you feeling?" I hear her, god knows after how much time. And I can't feel my body. It is a state of complete relaxation. I don't know if I have legs and arms. But I have a head and ears. I have a mouth, and it is dry.

"Is it all sepia? What do you see, Naina?" I hear her voice again. I am seeing an orange light. Everything is orange.

"Naina, what do you see? Is it all looking sepia to you?" she asks me. Her voice is echoing in my head.

"Yes," I mutter.

"Good. Now, move further into that sepia smog. It will feel like going into another world; walking through different stages of life. Keep floating and moving ahead. See how much further it takes you. It should lead you to the memory of another life." Her words echo around in my head. Strangely, she is right. It feels like walking into some other world. It is just... everything is in sepia tone.

"Do you see you?" she asks me.

"I didn't get you," I say, discovering that my own voice reverberates too.

"Naina, try to see the old you. The one you see in your dreams. Look for that lady. Think, and think only of her, and you will be taken to her." I do as she asked. I ponder on that lady. The snaps of my filthy dreams hover over my mind. I feel myself panting. All those images of me in Raghav's arms begin to torture me. I fidget in the recliner.

Suddenly, I hear a voice. A commanding voice of a lady. This voice is so familiar. I am drawn to it. My heart starts aching to hear it, as if I have a very deep connection with it.

I see that lady sitting in front of the mirror. Everything else is blurry. I start plodding towards her. She is the same woman from my dreams. I know this is all happening in my head. But how? How am I seeing all this? She can't see me. I can't touch anything. I am a ghost. How is it possible?

Shit! She looks exactly like me. She is beautiful and delicate. She is dressed in a *ghagra-choli* and lots of jewellery – old bangles, hefty anklets, thick waistband, and gold and pearl beads and clips in her braid.

I can't take my eyes off of her. Is she me? Am I looking at myself? Was this me? I keep ogling at her. I want to hug her, and tell her that I am her. She is me. She looks ethereal and thinner than me.

I look around. We are in a huge room of a palace. I look back at her, and find her crying.

"Naina, please keep describing whatever you are seeing," Dr Sujata asks. I can't believe all this. Am I actually here? I look at everything, and it gives me a familiar vibe. I have been here before. I have been here. I sob.

"Naina, why are you crying? Have you found yourself? Please follow my instructions or you'll get lost," she requests.

"She is crying," I say. "I mean, the old me, my doppelganger, I have found her. She is wearing a heavy ghagra and astonishingly beautiful jewellery. She looks like a princess. I can't believe my eyes. I was a princess in my previous birth. I move around to find something related to this era. This chamber has more sections, separated by heavy velvet curtains. I find a huge bed. It has four bronze-coloured pillars, and a soft-touch bed sheet.

"I hear another voice. I go there and find an ordinarily-dressed woman talking to the old me. This woman has broken some bad news to her, and she starts crying horribly. The other woman feels sorry for her too, but doesn't come forward to calm her.

"I see her wiping her face with a cloth and getting up, uprightly. Like she is ready to face her plight. She walks out of the chamber and I follow her. She is scooting pretty fast in her bulky ghagra, I notice.

"I see two more ladies, donned exquisitely, just like her, in regal jewellery and ensembles, outside the palace. One of the two is astonishingly beautiful. She looks fashionable. Her hair is knotted sprucely. Her jewellery looks exclusive. Her skin is sparkling, and her hair is brown. Who is she?

"And all three of them are crying. But none of them console each other.

"It seems like they are waiting for something. I hear the heavy beats of drums, and now the sound of trumpets. It is getting louder and louder. All three of them stop crying.

"A swarm of soldiers comes towards the big gate of the palace. The ladies are gathered on the podium inside the main gate. Is it men returning from a war? Have they lost somebody in the war?

"I see an elephant with somebody ensconced on it. He seems like a star of this place. Everyone is cheering him. I look at my doppelganger closely. Shit! She is married. She is a married woman. I look at the other two ladies. They are married women, too. Are they co-wives?

"Are they co-wives of this man? But why are they crying? He is unscathed. And why am I still hung up on this life?"

"You will find out, Naina," Dr Sujata's voice tells me.

"Oh my god!" I get numb. That is Veerain. That prince is Veerain. I was Veerain's wife in my last birth. He has just climbed down from that elephant, and is waving like a hero to his people. Did he have three wives in our last birth? Did I have to share him with other women?!

"Naina, Naina," Dr Sujata persists.

"That prince on the elephant is Veerain," I say. "My doppelganger takes a colourful *thali* from a *dasi*, with lit *diyas*, burning incense sticks, saffron, and a *kalash*. The ordinary-looking co-wife indicates to the *dasis* to rush to Veerain. They dash to the palanquin, just stopping near the elephant.

"I am dumbfounded to see Veerain. I can't take my eyes off of him. He is wearing a *sherwani* with gold work on it. He has a *pagari* on his head, with gems and stones. He is wearing *jutis* and tons of gold. Did people dress up like this all the time, during that period? Which century am I in? Is my mind making all this up?"

"Naina, it is not a fantasy of your mind. Tell me, how would your mind design the faces of the people you are seeing right now? You can observe them from so close. Please, focus on what is happening around you," Dr Sujata explains.

"A girl with a long veil comes with Veerain onto the podium," I continue. "My doppelganger is welcoming him in the traditional way with *arti* and *tikka.* Why is she doing it? There is no other prince here. Just the three of them to welcome him, along with this lady. She touches my doppelganger's feet. And she gives her the blessings to stay married always. Darn! Is she also Veerain's wife? Is she Veerain's fourth wife? Are we all his wives or what?

"They all are walking into the palace now. I am stunned. I want to know what is happening? What mess is this?

"Veerain is moving in another direction with his new wife. And all his other wives, including my doppelganger, disperse in different directions. I follow my doppelganger with a gloomy heart.

"I see her, sitting with dasis all around her, in a circle on the floor. So, this is why she was crying earlier. They are talking about Veerain. His name is Vikramajit. My doppelganger is Rani Durgavati. My name was Durgavati. They are gossiping about Veerain's new queen; that she is sixteen years old and soon, will charm the king. Now that the wars are over, he will be lost in the spell of her youth and beauty. She is not from a strong realm. She has been gifted to the Raja ji for freeing Ajaamgadh from the rule of Mughal Empire after the death of Prince Muhammad Azam Shah. Now, Veerain is not a viceroy of the Mughal Empire, but a king himself. The Mughal Empire is slowly losing its strength over the territories outside the Delhi Sultanate. All the kingdoms are rebelling to get their states free from the reign of Prince Bahadur Shah I.

"Oh God! I wish I had shown some interest in history in my school. I only know about Aurangzeb. And yeah, his successor was Bahadur Shah. But I know nothing more. So, am I in that period? Which century was it, the 17th or the 18th?" I ask Dr Sujata and Ruby.

"You are in the 18th century. Try to find out about your dreams, Naina." Dr Sujata's voice sounds like she is hovering over a well and I am deep inside it. Her voice is echoing between the tall, dark walls of the well and then, finally reaching me. But their voices are clear. I am feeling like a part of their coterie now. I want to hear the gossip.

"They are saying to my doppelganger, Durgavati, that she should have borne a baby by now. She has been married to the king for six years. Being the foremost queen of this realm, she has not given a baby to its throne. But both the other queens already have one son each. And now, when this new bride has come, she will blossom everywhere in the palace. She is the youngest of all. One dasi says that Raja ji is only twenty-six years old, and there are still more queens to come in the future. All of them laugh loudly."

No one cares about Durgavati's feelings. But I care for her feelings. Their comments are hurting her.

"Some of them are saying that Raja ji will go insane for his new bride. Others are stating that Rani Kamlavati will not let him slip away from her control. She keeps Raja ji captivated with her lustrous beauty. She will not let him get loose. I am guessing that they are talking about that beautiful queen of Veerain's. One dasi asks Durgavati, why doesn't she learn some skills of the *Kamasutra* from Rani Kamlavati? It is whispered this is how she keeps Raja ji so enthralled. Every time he comes back to the palace, he spends his first four nights with Rani Kamlavati. He gets knackered by her, then Rani Sukanya takes over him. And when Durgavati's time comes. By then, he is left with no strength and no mood." I can see how much pain Durgavati is in. She is seated like a bereaved wife.

"Naina, you need to move forward. Here, you will not get more information," I hear Dr Sujata's voice. And I couldn't care any less about it. I am dejected to see my miserable condition. She looks like a body without a soul. Her tears have dried out. Tears spring to my eyes, seeing myself in such a forlorn condition. Look at her eyes – they are so beautiful. Why couldn't Veerain see it? What does she not have?

"Naina, I can understand that you are hurt to see yourself in such a state. But we have to move forward. You have to look for Raghav, and his relation with you. Don't get carried away," Dr Sujata tries to console me and usher me forward.

"I want to know why Veerain treated me like this. It seems like it is about me and Veerain. Raghav is not even in the picture." I cry. I can't imagine going through the same pain in this life.

"Naina, you will not find the answer sitting there," Dr Sujata says, very sternly. "You are simply wasting your time." So, I get up and close my eyes in my imagination. I begin to feel myself moving. When I next open my eyes in my head, I see Durgavati sitting with Raja ji, in her chamber. I feel ecstatic. He is romancing her.

"I am seeing Durgavati with Raja ji in her chamber," I narrate loudly. "They are fondling. He came to her. Durgavati is blushing. They both look so perfect together. Why can't Veerain see that? Durgavati mutters something to him. She is asking him for a child. To this, he blushes, and plants a kiss on her lips." I am so ecstatic to see them together like this.

"He says to her that she understands him," I continue. "He has been very busy with state affairs. He was a viceroy to Emperor Muhammad Azam Shah. But now, he is a king. He has to look after his kingdom. He is the caretaker and protector of his people. His responsibilities have doubled.

"He says he is very satisfied with her conduct. She is a responsible and very understanding queen. She supports him. The other queens do not get this. They pester him to make love to them. They all just want him to give them attention, and care about their frivolities. He mostly fibs about their beauty and trivial matters of concern; but with Durgavati, he can be himself. He can sleep peacefully in her lap and, sometimes, talk interminably to her about his duties. She always helps him make the right choice. He caresses her face with his hand, bringing her head close to his lips and kisses her. Then, he closes his eyes and dozes off." And Durgavati seems perfectly happy to have him sleep in her arms.

"It's the height of impudence. She waited for him for so long, and he comes to her, speaks a few flimsy words and then falls asleep, completely satisfied. Look at her! She is so stupid. I was so stupid. She is massaging his head now, and he is snoring peacefully." I am burning with indignation for Veerain.

"Naina, don't sit there ogling at them," Dr Sujata orders stoutly. "Get up and search for Raghav." I try to do exactly as she commands, but I can't focus on Raghav. My mind is disturbed due to Veerain's insolent behaviour towards me. I want to know if he changes in the future.

"I see Durgavati standing in the balcony of her chamber. She still looks dejected and melancholic. I stand beside her. I can feel a very familiar vibe with this place. Like I still remember, somewhere in my mind, that I have been here. I can see the village from here; the market, full of people. Stalls along both sides of the passage, people vending artefacts on the ground, beautiful and colourful decorative pieces hanging all around, it's breath-taking. There are no buildings, just huts made of mud, grass and branches."

"I look at Durgavati. She is staring at something. There is a man dressed in a black dhoti, with a black turban on his head. He is holding a basket, and talking to the guards."

"Naina, I asked you to think about Raghav. You have spent one-and-a-half hours. We still don't know why you dream of him." Dr Sujata sounds disappointed. But she can't feel what I am feeling.

"Durgavati walks outside her chamber. She goes to a group of dasis and scolds them for not doing their work properly. It is all about Raja ji, about what would impress him. A swarm of dasis comes to attend her. Durgavati walks into the atrium, instructing each of them about their respective duties. I believe she is the only one in this palace who takes care of everything. Afterall, she is the senior-most queen.

"Rani Kamlavati enters, sprinting after her little boy in the atrium. She is scolding him for not listening to her. I look at Durgavati's face. It kills her from inside. She feels embarrassed in front of all the dasis; perhaps because they make fun of her that Raja ji doesn't make love to her. Which is true!

"She plods back towards her room with a hangdog face. And I catch some dasis laughing behind her back.

"A *dasi* comes pantingly, halting before Durgavati. But Durgavati disappoints her, and begins to walk again towards her chamber."

"Naina, you are simply wasting your time. You have forgotten why we initiated your hypnotism," Dr Sujata grouches.

"Okay, I am focusing on Raghav," I reply, closing my eyes and filling my head with those filthy dreams of Raghav and me. My heart starts thumping. Opening my eyes, I find myself in the same chamber. I didn't go to that eerie place. Is Raghav not related to me in this birth? I see a dasi talking to Durgavati. Durgavati tells her something, and she rushes out.

"I can't find Raghav. I have tried," I announce aloud.

"Okay, you are probably tired," suggests Dr Sujata. "It's been almost two hours. I'll wake you up now."

"Raghav...I see Raghav. That's Raghav!" I get breathless and pale to see him. That's Raghav. I start gasping for air, and my body convulses with fear.

22

"Naina, calm down. It is okay. He can't see you. Relax your muscles," I hear Dr Sujata say.

"He is Raghav. He is entering my chamber behind the dasi. He looks exactly like he looks in my dreams. He is wearing a black dhoti and a black turban. He has tattoos on his body. I am scared. He looks scary. What is he doing here, in my chamber?" I stutter.

"Naina, relax. He can't see you. He can't harm you. It is just your memory. All of this has had happened centuries ago." Dr Sujata's voice makes me feel safe and secure.

"He looks like a snake charmer," I say. "He has a basket with him, like the one shown in movies, in which snakes are kept. He is carrying a flute too. He looks very cunning. Durgavati is not even looking at him. She is talking to the dasi who brought him. His expression is not right. He is staring at Durgavati with utter wonderment, like he has never seen a woman before in his life. His eyes are full of lust.

"Finally, Durgavati goes to talk to him. He bows in respect. Now, she should get the idea that this man is wicked and be hurled out of the palace. She gets uncomfortable with his gaze, but does not say anything."

"What are they talking about, Naina?" Dr Sujata sounds alert.

"Black magic. The dasi is praising his work. She is saying that he knows some marvellous techniques in dark magic. He can get a person what he yearns. He bows again proudly, and with a smirk, upon being praised. Durgavati doesn't look convinced. She refuses to take any help from him. He comes forward, and speaks a riddle in Persian.

"Durgavati notices him closely now. She stands with her back upright and confidently, to show him who he is talking to.

"He is very confident about himself. He seems fiendish. He says that he knows what she wants, and that he can help her get it.

"Durgavati asks the dasi to take him out. Again he speaks, loudly, some riddle in Persian, stepping forward intrepidly. He says he sees sorrow in her eyes. She is lonely. She wants love, or else she'll die. And he can help her. He can make any person go bonkers for her. This is where Durgavati gets wide-eyed. He is smart. And Durgavati is naïve and gullible.

"That dasi leaves him alone with Durgavati to talk," I continue. "Durgavati is pondering over it. Everyone knows that Raja ji has four wives, and that Durgavati doesn't have a child. So, naturally, she would be depressed and gloomy. He is just taking advantage of her loneliness. He is boasting about his unbelievable mystical powers to spellbind anyone. *You fool, he is using that power on you right now.* She is listening to him intently, but not looking at him. She is lost in her grief and wants her dreams to come true, somehow. She has no idea what cost she will have to pay for this." I am dismayed.

"Naina, it is okay. It is good that now, you at least know what mistake you made in your past life that is still haunting you," Dr Sujata says, hovering over me.

"Durgavati asks him something in a low, dull voice. She wants to know if he can really make Raja ji fall in love with her. He smiles shrewdly. He takes another step forward. He says that he can do it in just one day. She asks him what he wants in return. He bows, and says that he only wishes for his powers to be useful to his queen. He is hoodwinking his real intention." I am getting restless.

"Naina, what does Rani Durgavati say?" Dr Sujata sounds alarmed.

"She has agreed to do anything in return. I see a gleam in her eyes. She has become hopeful to get her Raja ji back. She is looking like a child, so naïve and so innocent." I sob. "Dr Sujata, my heart is scared for what is going to come. I want to get up now. I can't see myself in his arms, getting butchered."

"Naina, relax. Calm down. You have come so far. We are just a few minutes away from knowing the truth of your haunting dreams."

I try and focus. "Durgavati is asking him what she will have to do for it? He says she will have to visit his chamber, two nights before amavasya. That dasi, who brought him here to her, knows his place. He tells her that she should come at night, when it is dark outside and the markets are vacant. She is unnerved by this, and asks him why? He says if she wants to make Raja ji pine for her, then she will have to do as he asks. She is so dumb. How can she trust a stranger like that? Who will come to save her, when nobody knows her whereabouts? Can't she think through this?" I am agitated with her now.

"She agrees to it. He bows and leaves the room. I literally served myself up to him on a golden platter. I know what is going to happen there in his underground chamber." I blow up.

"Naina, go to Raghav's chamber that you see in your dreams." Dr Sujata says. "You are scared of visiting it again, that's why you are not able to reach that place. Don't be afraid. He can't harm you."

"I don't want to go there. Please, wake me up. I am done with this therapy. We all know what is going to happen now," I say dispiritedly.

"Naina, you are not getting it. These dreams are trying to make you aware of your mistake. They are guiding you. So that you don't repeat your mistake again in this birth." She speaks earnestly. I give it a thought. Raghav and Veerain... both are related to me from my previous birth. Raghav is insanely mad for me in my present life. And Veerain is my husband in both births. Guruji said that my lover worshipped Lord Shiva in his previous birth, to make me his wife in this life and that I'll marry him. According to this prophecy, Veerain is my lover. But Raja Vikramajit doesn't seem to be in much love with Durgavati. Would he really devote his life to Lord Shiva to get her in his next birth?

"I want to continue," I say, finally. "I am concentrating on that place now." I close my eyes in my head and think of that dark, grimy place full of snakes. I imagine Raghav's face – and quickly, feel the change in the environment around me. I feel cold.

"It is dark," I say. "Durgavati is with that dasi. She is asking Durgavati to walk down a passage, which will take her to an underground chamber. The dasi tells her not to scream or react upon seeing any snakes along her way. It gives her goosebumps and she asks the dasi to come along. The dasi says she can't, but she had gone down there before for her work, and it all worked out wonderfully for her. She assures Durgavati that she will get Raja ji's love after tonight, and that she deserves it.

"She leaves Durgavati outside the opening of a cave, with an oil lamp in her hand, standing alone amidst the dark night. I can see her quaking. I have no idea how I ever embarked upon that journey then, on my own and alone in the dark. All this for Veerain? For my love for him? I paid too much of a price to get his attention and love.

"Durgavati is so scared that she is not looking at the walls of the cave, fearing that she might catch sight of a nerve-racking creature. I become alert as I can hear the sound of water splashing, some distance ahead of us. We both turn left, following the path of the turning tunnel, and it opens out into a big chamber. Durgavati sees a snake before her, and drops the oil lamp. It shatters, and its glass pieces shine on the mud. But the place is lit enough to see everything clearly. There are mashals all around, burning on the walls and on the ground in their stands. Durgavati is scared stiff. Raghav wades through the pond towards us. He is bare-chested, with a black dhoti draped around his waist.

"I am retreating, but Durgavati is standing stiff. She thinks he is going to help her in restoring the long-lost love of her husband. Tears spring to my eyes. I was so innocent. How easily I believed him. He stands before her, bowing in respect, and then asks her to follow him. He kicks his snakes gently away, on his way to a big rock. He asks Durgavati to sit on it, and she does quietly. She is really scared, but pretending to be strong. I can't stay here any longer. My heart is aching at seeing my innocence being slashed. Can I wake up?" I ask. I am crying again now.

"Naina, I know it is hard for you. But we are very close. I want to know why has this snake charmer taken birth around you again? Why are these memories still haunting you?"

I know she is right. But it is really hard. "Durgavati asks him what she is supposed to do. He sits on the ground and smiles foolishly. He starts speaking with a smirk that it is going to be very hard for her. He asks her if she is determined to go for it. She says, she could walk on a path of burning coals right now, if it would get her, her love back. He says that she doesn't know yet about the sacrifices one has to make, to impress the Lord of Darkness. She says she is ready to do anything, never mind the sacrifice. He continues to smile, and asks, with his head bowed, if she is ready to sacrifice her chastity.

"On this, Durgavati gets on her feet immediately. He stands up, too.

He speaks, "Yes, if you want to make someone fall in love with you deeply, then you will have to sacrifice an equally big price."

"She does not say anything and steps back. He guffaws and says he knew already that she would not do it. He knew that she would not be able to sacrifice everything to earn her husband's love. He asks her to return and forget all about Raja ji. She will never get his attention and love in this life, and he is sure about this. She will keep yearning for his love throughout her entire life, and then one day, she will die, as alone as she has always been.

"Durgavati turns her face away from him. She is crying. Raghav doesn't say anything more, and goes back into his pond. But Durgavati doesn't leave. She is ruminating upon it. I want to hold her hand and take her out from this shitty place. But she sits back on that rock, and hides her face with her hands. Raghav blares from the pond that she has only tonight, and that she is thinking too much. No one would ever come to know about it, and many other women had done this with him to show their devotion to the Lord of Darkness. It will end soon and there is no use taking time to ponder on it. This is the only price she has to pay, if she wants her whole life to change.

"She gets up and looks at him, pensively. He asks her to doff all her clothes in the corner there, and to leave only jewellery on her body. He hints to a place for her to go to. No, no. Please, stop! No!" I bawl.

I feel somebody rubbing my shoulders. "She acquiesces to do what he asked. I can't narrate any more. I can't. I am sorry." I break down.

"It is okay, Naina. You can move farther, and see how long it goes on for," Dr Sujata suggests.

"I have moved away. But Durgavati is still there with him in the pond. I don't know how long it has been since then. He has removed her jewellery, some of it. I don't think she is in her senses... I am moving ahead again.

"She is still here; but now out of the pool. This place has grown darker in the meantime. All the mashals have now burned out. There are truckloads of ashes. It can't have been just one night. Shit! How long has she been here? And she doesn't seem to be in her senses. He's bewitched her. I am panicking now. It's been so long. What shall I do?!" I cry out.

"Naina, inspect that place. Look around. You will surely find something to get the track of time," says Dr Sujata.

"This place is horribly dark," I mutter. "I can't see much. There is a ray of light, though. It is very slender, and coming from outside."

"A ray of light," intones Dr Sujata. "Where would light come from in the night? It is morning, then."

"Yes, it is morning, then. When will he leave her? I am moving ahead."

"She has woken up," I say. "She is dressing in the corner. He is burning wood to light the chamber. She emerges feebly out of the darkness, and walks towards the tunnel. She does not look back at him. He doesn't say anything. He looks at her – like a mistress looks at her master. His face is telling me that he will not let go of her easily now. Durgavati has already walked out, so I am rushing back to her. Outside the cave, it is very bright. A new day, with the scorching sun hanging overhead.

"Everyone will notice her now. She changes her way and takes the jungle road to reach the palace. She is walking and walking –

until finally, she collapses. No one is here to help her. Her foot is bleeding. But somehow, she gets up again.

"She reaches a temple. She goes inside, to rest maybe. She sits beside a pillar. It is a *Shivalaya*. She closes her eyes and dozes off. What shall I do now?" I ask Dr Sujata.

"Move ahead," she suggests.

"I see her donned in simple village clothes. I think she didn't return to the palace and has gotten settled here. She is living in that Shivalya. She is eating offerings given by the people. She looks as good as a dead body. Her life became more miserable, in an effort to make it better. I don't know how long she has been living here.

"I hear the temple priest talking to a lady, saying that she came here a week ago, on the day next to amavasya. She has been here for a week, and nobody came looking for her. She is a bloody queen. And nobody gives a f**k about it. She should end her life now. Who is she living for?"

"Naina, Durga went to that temple the next day after the amavasya? But she went to that cave one day before the amavasya. Then, where was she for two days?" Dr Sujata asks me.

"I don't know," I say drearily. "She came here as soon as she woke up the next morning. I think she is atoning here."

"Naina, she was there in that cave for three nights, not one!" Dr Sujata hollers.

"Dear god! Really? Does Durga know about it?" I exclaim. "Wait! I see soldiers coming in here. They come and hover around her. She gets up... and they bow to her. Wait! Raja ji is also here. Durga gets stunned to see him, and tears spring to her eyes. He looks very, very worried and sick. She wipes her tears, and he holds her shoulders, gaspingly. Like he has been looking for her for a long while, and now his body has warmed up having finally found her. He asks her in desperation why did she abandon his palace and come to live here like an ascetic? She is tongue-tied. He hugs her.

"He says that he has come to take her back with him, and also apologises for his impassiveness towards her. After she'd left without giving him any notice of her whereabouts, he realised her worth in his life. He could not bear her absence, and he sent his soldiers to look for her in every direction. But he was looking in the wrong places. He thought that she had gone back to her hometown in anger. He didn't expect that she'd gotten so disheartened that she renounced the world and came to live in a temple like a hermit.

"He says he wants to live with her now." I wonder how he felt her absence in spite of his three other wives, including that youngest and newest one, and Rani Kamlavati, who has dominance over his heart. "He takes Durga to the palanquin and helps her to climb into it."

"Did Raghav's magic really work for her?" I ask Dr Sujata.

"I don't think so, Naina. He kept Durga there for three nights in his chamber. He tricked her into sleeping with him. He took advantage of her misery and loneliness. I think it is only Durga's care and pure love for Vikramjit that made him realise his love for her."

"He is staying with Durga in her chamber," I continue. "All the dasis are appalled to see this sudden change in Raja ji's behaviour. Durga has a different glow on her face. She is so happy. Raja ji tells her what he wants to eat, and she gives the order to the rasoi-ghar maharaj to cook it.

"Today, all the other ranis are cooking Raja ji's favourite food, with the maharaj in the rasoi-ghar. Rani Kamlavati is exasperated with Durga. She is staring at her with abhorrence. Nevertheless, Durga's life seems perfect now." I speak at last with contentment.

"Naina, what about Raghav? What is he doing now?" Dr Sujata sounds tensed and baffled.

"Durga is with Raja ji right now. He is making love to her, and she looks so satisfied in the moment that if she died right now, she would depart from this world peacefully. And I am moving forward now to know why Raghav is after me in this life."

"I see him. He is in Durga's chamber. What is he doing here? How did he come in here? Durga is asleep with Raja ji, and he is here. He is ogling at her sleeping with Raja ji. How did he sneak in?

"He is not alone. He's brought his monstrous snake too into her chamber in the darkness of the night. He takes out a roll of something, and places it near Durga's head. And then he walks away... with his snake following him. Oh, dear god! He will not let her live. He is planning something evil." I start panicking.

"Naina, relax. All of this has already happened. You can't do anything now to change it. You can only save your present life from getting ravaged by Raghav. So, move ahead. See, what he is up to."

"In the morning, Durga finds that roll beside her. She is unrolling it. It is a long sheet of paper. She takes it and runs to the other section in the chamber. I move to stand behind her and peep into it.

"It is like a letter. It is in Hindi. It is written by Azam. So, his name is Azam. It says that he wants to meet her again. That she must leave the palace and come to meet him, tonight. He will be waiting for her. If she does not follow his words, then she will have to pay a humongous price for it.

Oh, good god! Why is he calling her now? What for? She rolls it back up and burns it with a lit diya." I get goosebumps.

"This is what we wanted to know. This is your answer, Naina. Move forward and see what she does," Dr Sujata says.

"It is dusk outside. Durga is yelling at the top of her lungs at that dasi who brought Azam here. Durga is threatening to chop off her head along with Azam's. She is asking her to tell that mutt to think of his head. He is only a snake charmer. She can get his head chopped off for any stupid reason, without letting anyone ever know about it. He should not forget who he is dealing with. She is the queen. Her voice is shaky while screaming. After the dasi leaves, tears cascade down Durga's cheeks, and she drops to the floor. I think she is feeling remorseful for what she did."

I continue moving forward. "She is still crying in her bed. It is night now. Raja ji hasn't come. Shit! She is alone in her chamber. What if that bastard comes to her chamber again."

I move forward. "It is another night. Raja ji is asleep in bed, and Durga is sitting near the open windows, with the curtains tucked to the sides. She is staring into the vagueness. She looks sick. I don't think she has been sleeping and eating."

I am moving ahead. "Raja ji is here with her. He is romancing her, but she looks disinterested. He asks her what is troubling her, but she starts crying. Oh shit! Is she going to tell him everything? He will abandon her then. She does not speak, just continues crying horribly. He asks her if it is about a child – then says he is trying to impregnate her, but she is not helping enough. She laughs, hearing this. He laughs, too, and starts kissing her. They are making love."

"I am worried about Raghav. I am focusing on him now."

"He is here. Dr Sujata, he is here in Durga's room. He has his snake in his hand. It is forbidding and cruel. Durga and Raja ji are in deep sleep. Azam, or Raghav... whatever, his eyes are red. His face is full of hatred and anger. I have seen this face before. Raghav had this exact expression on my engagement day.

"He is walking towards Raja ji. I want to wake up Durga. What shall I do?" I bellow.

"His snake bites Raja ji! Dr Sujata, his snake has bitten Raja ji." I holler.

"He is going to Durga's side now. He takes out a roll, setting it beside her head again. Now he is walking back, but his snake is still in the chamber. His snake doesn't follow him." My heart is pulsing at its maximum rate.

"Azam nudges a copper bowl to fall on the floor. And he vanishes, waking up Durga. But Raja ji doesn't rouse. Durga sees Azam's snake crawling on the floor and screams.

"She shakes Raja ji breathlessly. But he is not responding. The snake crawls to the other section. She pleads for Raja ji to get up. But he is still not answering. She finally steps down, picks up a lantern and goes to Raja ji. She tries again to wake him up. But he is not rousing. She realises that Azam was here. She sees that letter of his in her bed – and rushes to it. "She is unrolling it. It says that Raja ji will die tonight, if Azam's snake doesn't suck its poison back from Raja ji's body. His snake will do so only if she goes to meet Azam. She has time until sunrise." How could you, Raghav?

"Durga starts inspecting Raja ji's body. She finds the snakebite above his wrist, on the right hand." Oh shit! Veerain will die. I am scared.

"She drops the lamp and starts crying."

I am crying too. Veerain will die. He will die because of me. I let that beast enter into our lives. I am the one who has spoiled everything.

"The snake emerges and stares at Durgavati, as if telling her to go to his master. Durga runs to the balcony. There is still time left for sunrise. She pours bowls of water on Raja ji to wake him up, but nothing works. She scoots out of the chamber. I follow her. There are guards outside. But what are they for? Azam was still able to enter in. They ask Durga if everything is fine. But she runs along the corridor, perplexed.

"I think she is wondering if someone can be called for help. Why doesn't she call their royal vaidya or raj guru? She comes dashing back to the chamber, and finds the snake perched in the middle of the chamber. She sees the time again on the balcony and then lights several diyas.

"What is she planning to do? She begins writing with a quill pen on a thick sheet of paper. She finishes writing, rolls up the sheet, and puts it next to Raja ji.

"Oh! She wrote him a goodbye letter? But why? Is she going to Azam? She stares at the snake, and then, she drapes a shawl around her upper body. She walks out and tells the guards that she is going for a stroll. They don't have to follow her, just come to her if Raja ji calls out for her."

"Naina, move forward," Dr Sujata tells me.

"She is struggling to find her way to his cave. The sun is about to rise soon." I am moving forward. "She has reached the cave. Why is she doing this? It is suicide. She can go to her village at her parents' house. How can she be so sure that Raghav, or Azam, would really revive Raja ji? What if he gets a hold on her, and Raja ji dies? It will all end. I was so dumb in my last birth. I created this mess.

"She enters the chamber, and he is there, honing his *kukri*. He gets so happy to see her. What does he think? That he can make her fall in love with him?

He finally speaks up, saying that he has fallen in love with her, and he can't live without her. He knows that this is wrong on his part to forcibly call her to his den, threatening to kill her husband... but he had no choice. He tried to forget her. But he couldn't. And then, he could not bear to see her with another man. He loves her, and he needs her. He, too, can give her all the happiness in the world.

"Durga is not reacting. She is only listening to him, standing still like a dead body. He is literally begging her to accept his love. So, this is his thing: begging. He has been doing this since his last birth.

"Durga walks in and sits down on the rock. She asks him if his snake would have sucked the poison out of Raja ji's body by now? Hearing this, he bursts with rage. What? What was he expecting? That after listening to his impassioned speech, she would go mad for him? He says that the next morning, she will leave this village with him.

"Holy crap! No! Durga is horrified. She joins her hands, begging him to let her go. She tells him that she is a Hindu, and that she has already married a man. A woman in her culture marries only once. Now she will die as Raja Vikramajit's bride only.

"He says that marriage and all of that is for fools. He believes in the bond of souls. And their souls are attached to one another. He has felt that connection. He feels attached to her. His world is different. He doesn't need to marry her to keep her with him till eternity.

"Durga says that she will die without Raja ji. He is packing his stuff already and bawls that she will gradually forget Raja ji. He will bind her soul with his forever, and that way, both of them will stay together... even after this life.

"Durga runs to the tunnel. But his snakes come in her way. Azam doesn't even react to this attempt. He says that as soon as she starts cooperating with him, her life will become easy. Now, he is her master. Azam begins feeding his snakes and asks Durga to sit comfortably on the rock. He promises that soon he will build a palace for her. He will bring jewels and gems for her. She is his only priority now. With his magical powers, he will work to solve people's problems, and demand gold coins in return. He asks her to trust him.

"She retorts, solve problems the way he did hers? He has almost packed his stuff. Durga is searching for a way out. His snakes hiss at her. But Azam shushes them, asking them to behave respectfully with her. He is demented. He talks to snakes.

"She is not able to find a way out." I feel my body convulse due to distress, fiercely.

"Naina, relax. You are in the 21st century. There is no Azam here. There is no Durgavati. You are happily married to your lover Raja Vikramajit. His name is Veerain. Naina, Veerain is fine at home, waiting for you. Raghav is not even in India. You are safe and secure."

Dr Sujata calms me.

"Fire! There is a fire. Everything is burning!" I shout. "Durga is scared. Azam's snakes are burning. He is rushing to save his snakes.

"Raja ji's army is lighting the fire. They are here. How did they come here? I spot Raja ji too; he is stomping angrily towards Azam.

"He grabs hold of Azam's head by his hair, and kicks him down onto the ground. Two soldiers clench him from behind. Raja ji takes out his sword from its scabbard, and raises his arm high into the air. A soldier bends Azam's back from behind, to make him bow down. Raja ji brings down. His head flings down. Azam's body is fidgeting, and then, finally, lands heavily onto the ground, throwing mud into the air.

"Raja ji wipes off the blood from his face. He is looking fine now. How did he come here? He starts searching for Durga in the smoke. I am still looking at Azam's body. Blood is spurting out of his neck and mixing into the soil.

"Soldiers start running out. The air of the cave has begun to fill up with suffocating smoke. Everyone is coughing badly. Where is Durga? Raja ji and his soldiers are all looking for her... but I spot her instantly. She had run into a corner. She is choking.

"I see Azam's kukri in her hand. No, Durgaaaa! She has stabbed herself in the belly. I rush to Raja ji. He is looking in the wrong places. His soldiers ask him to move out. They are saying they will find the Rani Sahiba. Raja ji collapses onto the ground.

"A soldier finds her, and calls out loudly to Raja ji and the other soldiers. She is crying. She is in pain. Raja ji comes running and sits with her on the ground. He takes her in his arms, commanding a few soldiers to bring the Raj vaidyas. He starts crying. I thought he would be mad at her, but he is not. He is hurt to see her in pain. She wants to say something. I don't think she can keep her eyes open for long. He asks her, why? Why did she do this?

"She replies, saying how could she face him now? She doesn't deserve to live. Dying is now better for her than living. But she is happy, because she had never thought that she would die in his arms. She'd always thought that she would die alone in her chamber. But now she is peaceful.

"He cries. He hugs her. He says that he loves her. She has always been there for him, and he failed to acknowledge it. He realised her worth very late. She asks him if he loathes her now. He tells her that he can never do that. When he read her letter, he thought of only protecting her from that devil. He thought that he would lose her forever... and now, he is losing her.

"He begs her to stay, to keep her strength and live with him. But she says repeatedly, not in this birth. But she wants a promise before she closes her eyes forever. He asks, what can he give her now?

"She is not able to speak. She is going. What is her last wish? He bawls her name loudly, and she opens her eyes."

"She says, 'marry me'. She asks Raja ji to marry only her in the next birth. He looks at her in astonishment and then says he will. He will become a hermit now, and spend his entire life in penitence for breaking her heart. He will devote his life austerely to Lord Shiva, and ask him to make her his one and only wife, in his next birth. She smiles and closes her eyes."

Epilogue

Rani Durgavati's Letter

Raja ji

I have always loved you. You know that in my life, the only person who matters the most to me, is you. I left my parents' house six years ago. Now, even their existence does not matter to me as much as yours does. I have prayed for your health and victory day and night. I have cried all day long, wishing for your survival. You know I have always stayed loyal to you. But I made one mistake. One very big and unforgivable mistake, which can't be revealed. One mistake, after which I have lost the right to be called your wife. After which I have lost right over your love. I slept with another man. I slept with a snake charmer in his cave near the Shiva Temple, in the forest. He fooled me. He promised me that he knows the occult, and could make you fall in love with me. I believed him. He called me to his cave and asked me to sleep with him in return for his service. I could have left from there, but I slept with him. He came back a few days ago and asked me to go to him again. I didn't. Tonight, he came again, and had you bitten by his poisonous snake. I have time only till sunrise to save your life. I am going to him. And I will never return. If I get a chance, I'll end my life tonight. I soiled your impeccable image. I am a whore. I am not a queen anymore. But I have loved you with all my heart, and never thought of any other man in my dream, let alone in my life. I now wish that I had killed myself that night, instead of sleeping with him. I wish I had died long ago, because I could never do anything for you. I could not give you a child, or any pleasure in life. May you live long! I have always loved you.

Durgavati, the bane of your life

What happens next...

I couldn't speak a word. Thank god Ruby was with me. She brought me to her house. She talked to Dr Sujata after the session, because I couldn't speak a word.

Ruby is asleep now. Her bedroom is dark. I lay down in bed first, asking her not to disturb me. I pretended to sleep.

What happened today? Was all that for real?

I can't stop my tears. I can't breathe. How will I live with the baggage of my past life mistakes? I slept with another man. I slept with Raghav. And Veerain still loved me. He still worshipped Lord Shiva to marry me in this birth. Why did he come to save me? He shouldn't have come. He should have let me die alone, in a miserable and wretched condition in Raghav's cage. I don't deserve Veerain. And I'm doing the same thing all over again. My despicable dreams are a proof of my debauched character.

I check Wikipedia again on my phone. Ajaamgadh did exist in the province of Uttar Pradesh back in the 18th century. Its viceroys include the ancestors of Raja Vikramjit. After Raja Vikramjit became a hermit, kingship continued through the son of Rani Kamlavati.

There is even a mention of me as the first queen of Raja Vikramjit, who had not borne a child and died early. And that after the demise of Rani Durgavati, Raja Vikramjit left his throne for his eldest son, and became a recluse.

Acknowledgements

This novel wouldn't have seen the light of day without the encouragement and support of my mother, father and brother. They showed tremendous faith in me and my passion to become an accomplished author. Whenever I felt demotivated, my brother helped me pull myself together by infusing in me confidence to make my dreams come true. Mumma has always been there by my side with her assuring smile, saying, "You can do anything." I want to thank my Mumma and Papa for giving me their immense support.

At last, the ones who made all this possible for me are team Srishti Publishers. Srishti provides guidance, hope and a platform to budding authors and hugely supports their work. That's why many authors who were given their first chance by Srishti Publishers are renowned today.

My special thanks to Arup Bose, Stuti and the entire team of Srishti for their warm hospitality, cooperation and hard work on this book.